# Contents

*Janice Wallander*

## A Novella Retelling the Tale of Rumpelstiltskin

Novella One of *After the Tales and Princesses- A Set of Novellas*

**Aleese Hughes**

ISBN: 9781696259095

**Dedication**

To my beautiful mother, for editing *everything*! From school papers to short stories, and now my books! Thanks for being the loving, selfless person that you are.

# Before you Read

This novella is about a character from the first book of *The Tales and Princesses Series*. For best enjoyment, *Peas and Princesses* (Book One) should be read before this novella.

# Chapter 1

Bavmorda knocked on the splintering door before her. The little cottage was rather battered and rather broken. Not something she would have liked to live in— not that she really lived anywhere nowadays.

The door opened with an ear-splitting creak. Bavmorda was surprised the rusted hinges of the door didn't pop right off. Standing before her was a homely-looking, young man. His pale, blond hair was disheveled, and his tunic was so baggy it was falling off his narrow shoulders.

Bavmorda crinkled her nose. "*You're* the sorcerer spinning straw into gold? Not what I expected."

The boy folded his arms in contempt. "And you are?"

Bavmorda ignored his question and pushed past him and into the home— if one could call it that. She surveyed the room for somewhere to sit. There was dust piled up about an inch high on the floor and every other surface. The one chair in the room sat by a long-dead fire with its own pile of filth atop its seat.

"Good heavens, child!" she exclaimed. "What did

you do to this place?"

The young man snorted and shut the door against the chill, night air.

"It was like this when I found it."

Bavmorda looked eagerly at the cold coals in the pathetically tiny hearth and tightened her ratted shawl around her shoulders.

"You found it like this?"

He nodded and moved to sit in the single chair before Bavmorda got the chance to take it herself. She narrowed her eyes at him.

"I needed somewhere to stay," the boy said, picking at his fingernails. "This place was abandoned, so I claimed it."

"Ah, yes. You ran away from Greriveth when your father died."

The young man stopped staring at his nails. His eyes widened as he moved his head to look at Bavmorda.

"I ask again, who are you?" he demanded.

Bavmorda chuckled and flipped her few strands of brittle, gray hair behind her shoulder. "The name's Bavmorda. I'm a—"

"Witch?" he shouted, jumping from his chair and rushing over to her in excitement.

Bavmorda frowned. The fear and disbelief people usually felt from learning of her title was always the fun part. Why was this young man so thrilled about seeing a witch?

"I've heard of you!" he said, interrupting her thoughts. "You're a legend among us!"

"Us?" She raised an eyebrow.

He nodded fervently. "Where I trained in sorcery and magic. It was me and a few other students learning from a man named Doran."

Bavmorda's shoulders fell, and she sighed heavily. "Ah, Doran. He causes a lot of trouble."

Months ago, Bavmorda had provided that warlock with a warning about handing out poisoned apples, but just as soon as she had left, he had picked it right back up again. It seemed now she needed to do more than that to get through to Doran. Maybe that's where she'd head next.

"What?"

She waved the thought away. "Never mind. I'm here to ask why you've been boasting around this small village that you can spin straw into gold." She leaned forward and lowered her voice. "Most people in Mardasia don't even know magic is a real thing. Your boastings, especially outside of this village, might not be taken very kindly."

He merely shrugged at her, which only made her notice how scrawny he was. Bavmorda rubbed her face with her hands, exasperated.

"What's your name, child?"

The boy caught his breath. "Names aren't important."

Bavmorda licked her lips eagerly, pleased to have struck a sensitive chord in the young man.

"What if I told you I could guess it?" She wiggled her knobby fingers playfully.

He gulped. "I'd like to see you try." Though the

words were brave, his voice wavered.

Bavmorda cackled in her throat, then rocked back on her heels in deep thought, searching through the spells in her mind that would grant her what she sought. Then, with delight, she squealed.

"I could see why you don't want people to know your name, Rum—"

"Stop!" he cried, holding his hands over his ears. "I have a stupid, *stupid* name! Just call me Ronan."

It was the witch's turn to shrug. She had no place to talk when it came to changing and experimenting with a name.

"As you wish, Ronan."

Ronan sighed in relief and moved back to the chair.

"So..." he continued. "Is that the only reason you're here? To make sure I stop displaying my abilities?"

Bavmorda nodded. "That's about it. And to tell you to start traveling to Kria."

The young man furrowed his brow. "The capital of Polart? Why?"

Bavmorda began to walk away as he spoke but turned back and said, "You say you've heard of me. That I'm a legend. Maybe that means you should trust me. Now, if you'll excuse me, I have a *lot* to do."

# Chapter 2

Milly and her husband were off in Greriveth at a fabulous ball, and Janice was left to fend for herself alone in the castle of Polart. After Milly's marriage to Prince Alexander, and then becoming the Polartian Queen, both Janice and Milly knew they would hardly see each other if Janice didn't uproot her own life and move to Polart, as well. But in that moment, in a large castle without her sister's shining presence, Janice was starting to regret that decision.

Janice couldn't help but wonder if something was wrong with her as she missed Milly's and her little cabin in Marviton— especially as she roamed the magnificent halls of the castle. They sold the place to the merchant Bart soon after Milly's wedding. Had that really been six months ago? Though so much time had passed, it was still hard to believe her sister was a *queen*.

The Polartian castle was cold, and Janice began rubbing her bare arms with her hands to warm herself. Upon first arriving, she was able to appreciate the luxurious carpets and giant paintings hanging on every wall. And now, it all seemed unnecessary, and lately, Janice only thought of how cold it was. Milly had told her that she often missed the simplicity of their old life, but she was happy. And Janice was happy *for* her. Janice also knew that she could never leave her sister— Milly was the only family she had, and she wasn't about to live an entire kingdom away from her sister. Especially after the stunt King Leopold pulled in kidnapping Milly and fashioning her into a fake princess all those months ago.

Janice finally made it to the back of the huge building and stepped through the tunneled trellis that led to the castle gardens—the one place she felt she could relax. The gardens were expansive, going on for miles and were bordered along the edges with tall trees. She smiled at the hues of green leaves adorning the trees around her and the crisp smell of fresh air. Summer was a wonderful time of year in Mardasia, especially for plant life.

Janice's first sight of the gardens had taken her breath away, and she took any opportunity she could get to walk among the well-trimmed maze of hedges or read a good book by the pond that, in her mind, was big enough to be a lake. She strolled through the gardens a *lot*. It helped that Janice didn't have any responsibilities to attend to— she wasn't a monarch like Milly, and the servants took care of all the busywork at the castle. It actually drove her crazy to have nothing to do. She felt more like a nuisance than the Queen's sister, but Milly and Alexander would have a fit if she were hired among the kitchen staff. They wanted Janice to feel welcome and important.

Janice found a bench beside the pond that over-looked the quaint gazebo in the middle of the water. She sighed in relief as she sat, feet hurting from the long march from her rooms and to the outside. The air was crisper than the day before, and she regret-ted not bringing a shawl with her. Or, at least, she should have worn a longer-sleeved dress.

Thinking about clothes, she looked down at the ensemble she was wearing. It was an elegant, green silk that felt *incredible* on her skin, but the multiple layers of skirts were heavier than her simple frocks from home.

She shook her head. There was no point in dwell-ing on all the negative. Besides, there were probably hordes of people who would kill to be in her posi-tion. Janice let out a long breath of air, kicking her feet back and forth. They didn't even brush the grass below her— an obvious reminder to how short she was.

"Miss Wallander?"

Janice jumped up in fright, nearly tumbling into the water. After regaining her balance, she turned around to the familiar voice. Reginald, one of the castle stewards Janice only ever saw in passing, stood before her. His gangly form towered over her own by at least two feet and his graying hair was slicked back neatly.

"Oh, Reginald," Janice breathed. "I'm sorry, I didn't see you there."

His face revealed nothing as it remained flat.

"That's quite alright, miss."

Janice shook her head, mousy-brown curls whipping at her cheeks. "Please, I insist you call me 'Janice.'"

She lost count of how many times she had told the servants to call her by her first name. She could tell many felt uncomfortable with what she was... She wasn't a noblewoman by any means, but she *was* the Queen's sister. So they stuck with the "Miss Wallander"s, and the "misses."

"Miss Wallander," Reginald continued, ignoring Janice's invitation for a first-name basis, "I was sent to inform you that dinner is ready."

Janice flitted her eyes to the sky. The sun was throwing beautiful purples and oranges across the horizon as it began to set. She didn't realize how late it had become.

"Will you ask for it in your rooms again?"

She looked to the steward and paused. He raised an eyebrow at the hesitation but stood as stiff as before. Janice's thoughts were spinning as she tried to convince herself that she needed to be more social and try to enjoy herself, even if Milly was gone.

"No," she finally said. "I think I'll join the Regent, and the advisors today."

Reginald gave a curt nod. "As you wish, Miss Wallander."

# Chapter 3

The food was definitely something Janice couldn't complain about. In Marviton, it was mostly fruit and vegetables from their garden and a thin piece of meat about once a week.. At the Polartian castle, she was given *courses*. Salads with sweet dressings, soups that could fill her by themselves, and always a generous slab of meat served with a side of potatoes, carrots, and everything in between. Not to mention all the desserts. Janice could have sworn she had gained ten or fifteen pounds since living there. The extra weight didn't hurt anything, however. She didn't realize how scrawny she had been until interacting with the noblewomen of Mardasia and Polart alike. Janice was now able to admit to herself that instead of being bony, she had flattering curves.

Janice eagerly shoveled another bite of chicken into her mouth and chewed vigorously. But as she got one glare after another from the men and women eating around her, she flushed deeply and sank into her chair. She had never proven good at manners and etiquette.

"So, Miss Wallander?"

Janice lifted her chin to meet the eyes of the acting regent in Alexander's and Milly's absences. Edward was a younger man but still older than Janice. He was maybe in his late twenties, and she had just turned twenty-one. Though still in his youth, his dark hair had already begun to recede. He had a pointed nose that angled downwards like a crook, and his beady eyes made him look more mole-like than human.

"Yes?" She set her eating utensils by her plate. She wasn't going to embarrass herself by talking with her mouthful as she did on many other occasions.

"I was wondering if the King and Queen mentioned giving you a new title?"

All eyes were on Janice again. There were about three women and four other men surrounding her, advisors to Alexander and Milly. Each was dressed regally, and the women (and a couple men) had a pile of makeup on their faces. Janice tried rouge once at Queen Amelia and King Robert's coronation in Mardasia and refused to wear even a touch of makeup ever since. She didn't like how it felt.

"Um, new title? They didn't say anything..." She wrung her hands nervously under the lacy tablecloth. Why did she not stay in her rooms? The nobles always judged her, and she could never act in the way she was meant to.

*I wish Milly were here*, she thought. *She always makes me feel better.*

Edward nodded. "They decided it would make sense to name you a lady of the court."

Janice's jaw dropped to the floor, and she froze. What? A lady? She didn't quite know how to feel about the revelation.

The Regent cleared his throat after the silence grew for an uncomfortable amount of time. "It makes sense, does it not? You must agree, of course."

A part of her knew he was right, and becoming a lady would help with the "who she was" and "where she belonged" bit that confused not only her, but everyone around her. But the other part of her was holding onto her old, simple life. If she became a lady, there would be no chance of ever getting that back. She wasn't sure what she wanted.

"You're allowed to do that?"

Edward shrugged. "Queen Mildred was born a commoner. Look at her now. And if the King and Queen wish to bestow a title on you, no one can really stop them."

The advisors around them murmured in agreement. Janice was surprised. She had expected there to be more argument about the proposal, but any hesitation towards commoners entering the court must have dissipated when Milly became their Queen, and she was highly respected and well-loved by the people. It might have had a bit to do with the dictatorial queen they had before her...

"Miss Wallander, are you alright?"

Janice shook her head. "I'm sorry. I was just thinking."

The regent furrowed his bushy brows. "Oh? Well, will you accept the title?"

She forced a smile, but before she could accept, the massive doors of the dining hall whooshed open. A plump, short manservant with a neat pony-tail stood before them. At his side was a middle-aged man. His clothes were tattered, and he trembled violently.

"Regent," the servant said with a bow. "May I interrupt?"

Edward sighed and dropped his fork with a thud. "You already did."

The servant pursed his lips but took the words as an invitation to continue. "You might want to hear what this man has to say."

Janice took that as her cue to leave, but as she stood, Edward gestured for her to sit back down.

"It's okay, Miss Wallander. You can stay."

Janice slowly retook her seat as the manservant strode into the room, but the visitor hobbled behind much slower. He seemed to be limping.

"What is your name, and what is the need for your visit?" Edward boomed, louder than necessary. The trembling man took two steps backward in fear.

"My name is Lionel, R— Regent," he stammered. "And something terrible... in my village..."

Edward and many others in the room rolled their eyes.

"Get on with it," he snapped while staring down at his unfinished plate, obviously wanting to get back to other things.

Janice clenched her fists under the table. Lionel was obviously distraught. The least the Regent could do was show just a smidgen of kindness.

The man bowed deeply. "Apologies, my lord. My village, Bymead, was attacked not two days ago."

The advisors at the table rudely chattering soon quieted at the visitor's words. Edward rose quickly from his chair, the legs scraping loudly against the floor.

"By whom?"

Janice could see the lump in Lionel's throat bounce as he tried to gulp it down.

"Bandits, my lord."

"Bandits?" Janice exclaimed. All heads turned in her direction, and her hand flew up to her mouth. Had she said that out loud?

Lionel gave her a swift nod. "Yes, m'lady. They were definitely Polartian, and they stole *everything* — our crops, our money... We even—" His voice broke as he shifted his teary eyes to the floor. "There were a couple fatalities. My own daughter was one of them."

Janice gasped. "How terrible!"

But the Regent and many of the others around her were unfazed by his words. To them, it was normal news. Milly told her that bandit raids happened on occasion. Alexander and Milly were really good at showing compassion to the people and caring about their problems, so the Regent's reaction was disappointing to Janice.

"How many were among the bandits, do you think?" Edward asked while mindlessly pleating the tablecloth beside his plate.

"I'd say about twenty, my lord."

The Regent moved his hand to his chin, deep in thought. All in the room held their breaths in anticipation of what his reply might be.

"I could probably send an entourage of ten men from the royal guard," he finally said.

Janice furrowed her brow. That couldn't be enough...

Lionel seemed to think the same thing as his lip trembled in disappointment, but he thanked the Regent, anyway.

"I'll also send the physician's apprentice to attend to any injuries or other ailments if need be."

The visitor perked up. "Yes, lord. Thank you, lord."

Janice leaned back in her chair, thoughts spinning. She also had a little knowledge of medicine, her late mother having been skilled at such things. Janice had taken quite an interest in her mother's medicinal work before her death.

"R— Regent," she stammered.

Edward turned to her once again with a raised eyebrow. "Did you say something, Miss Wallander?"

She cleared her throat. "Uh, yes. I— I was thinking that I might go with the party, as well. Maybe I could be of help to the physician's apprentice. I know a little bit about medicine."

The Regent cocked his head as he studied her. "That's not a bad idea."

Janice's lips rose into a small smile at the subtle compliment. She had expected him to shoot down her idea immediately. The advisors, however, chattered nervously about sending the Queen's sister into danger. Edward held up his hand to attain silence once again.

"I think Miss Wallander traveling to help the village of Bymead is the perfect opportunity to prove herself to the people and justify becoming a lady of the court."

Janice lifted her chin with confidence. The Regent was right— she hadn't thought of that. A few murmurs of agreement echoed around her, and Lionel chimed in with his own gratitude for all the help he could get.

"It's settled then," the Regent said, slamming his palms onto the table with determination. "Those involved will leave straight away tomorrow morning."

# Chapter 4

Janice was thrilled for an opportunity to leave the castle. A small village with humble, ordinary people was just what she needed while Milly was away. And as she stood there waiting to get assigned a luxurious carriage, surrounded by ten intimidating men of the royal guard dressed in uniforms of the deep red and purple colors of Polart, she felt even more convinced of that need.

"You must be Miss Wallander," a high-pitched voice said behind her.

Janice craned her neck over her shoulder to find the source of the voice. A boy that couldn't have been any older than sixteen stood behind her with hands clasped behind his back. He was sickly-looking, with pale skin and sunken eyes. She could even count his ribs through the tight tunic he wore on his torso.

"I am," she replied. "And you are?"

. "I am the new physician's apprentice, miss. Egbert's my name."

Janice furrowed her brows in confusion. "New? What happened to Henry?"

Egbert smiled, revealing a row of yellowed,

crooked teeth. For a physician's apprentice, he didn't seem to care for himself very well.

"He was... not up to the job."

Janice drummed her fingers against her thigh. Something about Egbert's statement made her nervous.

"Well," she finally said. "It's a pleasure to meet you, Egbert."

Egbert gave a deep bow, embellished with a sweeping movement from his long arms. "Same to you, Miss Wallander."

She grimaced. "Please, call me Janice."

Egbert raised an eyebrow and peeked up at her from his bow. "Is that appropriate? You are the Queen's sister."

Janice rolled her eyes. "I know."

And with that, she turned on her heel and trudged away to the carriage a couple footman just pulled up. The large palfreys at the front whinnied and clopped their hooves, anxious to continue moving.

"Is this for me?" she asked.

One of the two footmen in the driver's seat gave a curt nod, white wig bouncing precariously on his head.

"Yes, Miss Wallander. This is actually for both you and the apprentice. It's just you two going. Well, except for the soldiers, of course. They'll be riding horseback as protection."

Janice's muscles stiffened. *Great*, she thought. *A long carriage ride with Egbert.* She had hoped for a little alone time. But it did make sense that more than one carriage would be superfluous when just two seats were needed.

"Wait, what happened to Lionel?" she asked, remembering the village visitor from the night before.

"He left right after his audience with the Regent."

"How delightful!" a squeaky voice cried behind her.

Janice jumped. Egbert seemed to have started creating a pattern of sneaking up behind her. He rubbed his hands together as he studied the ornate, golden frame surrounding the doors of the white carriage.

"We get to travel together! In luxury, might I add!"

Janice took in a sharp breath and forced a smile. "Yes. Delightful."

Egbert was very talkative, and Janice definitely was not. Not a great combination for a four-hour carriage ride. Her head began to pound after an hour of his constant conversation, and she closed her eyes and rested her head on the glass of the carriage window. It was hot from the summer sun, but she figured lying on the cushioned seat would be unladylike.

"I'm sorry. Am I boring you?"

Janice's eyes fluttered open to look at the boy across from her, realizing closing her eyes and resting her head while he was talking was rude.

"Oh, no," she lied. "I just have a headache."

"I've got just the thing!" he exclaimed, rummaging through the leather physician's bag next to him.

Janice rubbed her temples and inwardly groaned at his loud voice.

"Here! Freshly picked this morning." Egbert held out a sprig of peppermint. "If you lightly chew on a leaf, it should start helping. Also, the sm—"

"The smell should help on its own," she finished for him, graciously taking the plant from his hand.

Egbert sat back, amused. He placed a hand on his chin and scooted forward in his seat, studying her. "How much do you know?"

Janice shrugged as she took in a deep breath of the peppermint, welcoming the refreshing, cool scent as the soft leaves tickled her palm.

"What would you use to treat stomach pains?"

"Wormwood," she said without hesitation. And with further thought added, "Mint can help, as well."

Egbert nodded his head a few times. "Antiseptic for wounds?"

"Myrrh."

He sat back again, taking a long look at her. "You do know some stuff. That's good. I was afraid you just *thought* you did."

Janice pursed her lips, annoyed by his previous

assumptions, but quickly relaxed as she realized he was trying to give her a compliment.

Egbert and Janice lurched forward with a sudden stop, and Janice was able to hear the muffled whinnies as it surprised the horses, too.

Egbert pushed the door open to his left and peeked his head out. "Why have we stopped?" he shouted.

Wails of pain reached their ears the instant Egbert finished shouting. Janice leapt from her seat, pushed the boy aside, and barrelled out of the carriage. She rushed in the direction of the cries and found a middle-aged woman on her knees, rocking back on forth with a little boy in her arms. They sat on the side of the road, but still dangerously close to where horse riders and carriages might drive past. The little boy had a big gouge on his forehead, and scarlet blood dripped past his face and onto his ragged clothes.

"What happened?" Janice cried.

The woman raised her gaze, and Janice could clearly see the tears pooling and spilling out of her brown eyes.

"He's—he's after us," she stammered. "My son hit his head. Ronan here just barely got us away." She nodded up to a young man standing above her, hand placed comfortingly on her shoulder.

Janice stumbled two steps backward, not having noticed this Ronan before. She was too focused on the injured boy. She shook her head, frustrated by her hesitation, and leaned down to the child to check his vitals.

"He's still alive," she said with her fingers on his neck to feel his pulse. Warm blood began to stain her fingertips, but she ignored it. "Lay him on the grass."

The mother obeyed as Janice ripped a strip of green, silky fabric from her nice dress. The castle tailors could always make more dresses. She gathered the piece of cloth into a ball and pressed it against the child's wound.

"What are you doing?" the young man named Ronan asked.

"I'm staunching the blood," she replied.

At that moment, Egbert had sauntered to her side. She narrowed her eyes at his leisure attitude. A few of the guards in their entourage had approached with him, obviously nervous of the strangers' intentions to the Queen's sister and the physician's apprentice.

"He hit his head," Janice snapped to Egbert. "Do you have vinegar and some myrrh?"

Egbert's jaw dropped open at the blood, and his face grew a sickly green.

"Egbert!"

He shook his head, darting his eyes away from the scene. "Here," he said, handing his bag to her.

Janice clenched her jaw, frustrated that Egbert proved useless. "Ronan," she said, "hold the cloth down on his head."

Ronan bent over the boy and pressed against the wound with his scrawny arms. He looked as if he'd barely eaten in ages.

Janice scrambled to find a bottle of vinegar, commonly used by court physicians to clean wounds. Once her hand hit the glass, she pulled it out with fervor. Janice unstopped the cork to smell and determine if it really was vinegar. Satisfied, she directed Ronan to remove the cloth, and then she poured some of the liquid on the wound. The boy flinched, but his movement was a good sign. After patting it dry and assuring the blood had slowed, she found some myrrh and gently patted the cakey resin onto the cut.

"It's just a surface wound," she assured the mother. "Those tend to bleed a lot, that's why he's going in and out of consciousness. He might have a concussion, but the skull is intact. After I stitch him up, he should heal just fine."

The woman's lip trembled, and she threw her arms around Janice's shoulders. She smelled as if she hadn't bathed in weeks, and her shawl scratched against Janice's skin. But she didn't mind. Janice hugged the grateful mother back with a smile.

Janice moved to sew the wound closed, and as soon as the needle hit skin, Egbert rushed away and heaved until all of his lunch was piled onto the grass, not five feet away. Ronan wrinkled his nose in disgust.

"Obviously not a physician like you," he said to Janice.

Janice smirked, tying up the last bit of thread and handing the child back to his mother. "He *is* the physician. I just know a few things."

Ronan threw his head back and laughed. "Guess he's never been around a real injury."

Janice chuckled along with him and threw a look at the sick apprentice. "Guess not."

"Ma'am." one of the taller guards directed to the mother, who still sat on her knees as she rocked her son.

This guard seemed to be in charge of the entourage. The others listened to and respected him, and his uniform was slightly nicer than the others': there was gold trim along the hem, and the fabric was thicker. As Janice studied him, she noticed how regal and handsome he was  with thick chestnut hair and a sturdy build. She felt her face grow hot. *Not* the time to be thinking of such things.

"What happened?" he said.

The woman opened her mouth to speak, but her relieved tears were too great a challenge.

"Her husband was after them," Ronan said for her. "Helga and Michael here have been running from the capital for *days*."

The guard raised an eyebrow and fingered the sword at his hip. "You're from Kria?"

Helga nodded. "We— we—"

"Her husband is still there," Ronan continued for her. "He was an abusive man, and I found them trying to escape. I got them out of the city." His eyes shifted to the ground as he said the next part, "He found us yesterday, however. We were running, and I was carrying Michael." He nodded his head to the boy, who was starting to regain consciousness. "And I tripped over a rock and dropped him."

Helga whimpered as he told their story.

"If you would, ma'am," the guard directed to Helga, "we can help you. One or two of my men can take you to Kria, have the court physician give all of you further examination, feed you, give you a place to stay... and we can make sure that your husband is found and dealt with." He puffed out his chest confidently. "I assure you that we will provide complete protection until you can get back on your feet again."

The woman pulled her son tightly to his chest. "I can't go back to my husband," she whispered. "I can't let him find us."

The guard squatted down next to her and didn't take his eyes away from hers. "I promise that won't happen."

"Why give us so much special treatment?" she demanded.

He chuckled. "The King and Queen would be very upset if we didn't help those in need, like yourself."

The woman crinkled her eyes up in a smile. "They're good people— King Alexander and Queen Milly. What's your name, sir?"

"You can call me Emmett." The guard outstretched a hand to help her up. She took it, son still balanced in her other arm. She was stronger than she looked.

Egbert shuffled next to the group and cleared his throat. "Excuse me," he directed to the guard.

Emmett lifted a strong brow at the apprentice, but then his face softened. "You should go to Kria with them," he said, saving the boy from embarrassing himself by asking for it. "They might need treatment on the way home."

Egbert paled and shifted his gaze to his feet. "What about Bymead?"

Emmett nodded his head at Janice. "She has proved more than capable."

"It would be an honor," Janice said, pleased by the compliment.

"Bymead?" Ronan asked. "What happened in Bymead?"

"It was attacked," one of the other guards standing a short distance away contributed.

Ronan's mouth dropped open. "Why? How?"

Emmett shook his head. "We don't have a lot of time to explain. Janice, Bymead is not far from here on steady horseback. Would you feel okay riding with me, and allowing the carriage to be given to those returning to Kria?"

Janice rose from her position and brushed the dirt from her torn dress. "Of course," she said. "I don't mind one bit."

"Can I come with you?" Ronan inched closer to Janice, reaching an arm out and grabbing hers. His eyes pleaded. "Please. I hate to think that people were hurt. I'd like to help."

Emmett and the other guards hesitated, but Helga fervently vouched for him.

"Do you know anything about medicine?" Janice

asked.

"Or fighting?" Emmett chimed in.

Ronan thought for a moment, finger scratching at his patchy scruff. "Well, I can promise that I will be of help in many ways. I'm an okay swordsman and a good listener." He looked at Janice. "I'll do whatever you ask me to do."

Janice slung Egbert's physician's bag over her shoulder and gave a curt nod. "I'd welcome the help if it's alright with everyone else."

Sounds of agreement spread through the group.

"Alright, then," Emmett said. "Let's all get going."

# Chapter 5

"This stop needs to be quick!" Emmett shouted to the group.

The guard sat directly behind Janice on the tall destrier they rode together. She felt the air he exhaled as he spoke tickling her ear. Janice couldn't deny the flutterings of her heart as she felt his warm breath on her neck and his strong arms wrapping around her to clasp the reins. She'd never been this close to a man before...

There were eight men left, including Emmett—who Janice rode with— so there were eight horses. Ronan rode alongside the horse she straddled with one of Emmett's men.

Once the entire party had pulled their horses to a stop by the side of the dirt road that had begun to narrow and led directly to a small brook, Emmett slid as far back as he could from me, then cautiously (so as not to kick me in the head) swung both of his legs over the saddle and hopped out with one fluid motion. He then held out an arm for Janice to take.

"Would you like to stretch your legs, Miss Wallander?"

Janice flushed as the guard flashed her a blindingly white smile. She nodded and took his hand gingerly. He pulled her out of the saddle, but as her feet hit the wet dirt below, she nearly lost her balance and fell against him.

Emmett smelled strongly of leather and steel, and for a moment, she felt lost in the scent. Janice leaned into his broad chest a second too long, then pushed herself away quickly.

"Thanks for catching me," she muttered with her eyes directed to her feet.

"Anytime!"

As soon as Janice looked up once again, Emmett had already begun to stride away with the other soldiers. The boisterous group seemed to be heading towards the bubbling brook to fetch some water for the horses. She grumbled under her breath, chastising herself. She wasn't there to fawn over and flirt with the royal guard. They were all there for a purpose.

The embarrassment she felt from the encounter was so much that she didn't notice Ronan approaching her from behind.

"Hey."

She whirled around, arms flailing, and the young man had to dodge the flurry of movement from her hands to avoid getting hit.

"Whoa, I just wanted to say 'hello.'"

Janice threw a hand to her heart and let out a long breath. "Sorry. I was deep in thought, I guess."

The young man grinned and wiggled his eyebrows at her. "Did this 'thinking' have anything to do with one Sir Emmett?"

Her face grew hot, and she began to pleat the fabric of her dress. "No."

He winked, but she shrugged any of his accusations away.

"Was there something you wanted to talk about?" she asked, changing the subject.

"I wanted to properly introduce myself." Ronan stuck a long arm out for her to shake it. "You know, since we'll be working together for the next little while."

Janice took his hand in hers and shook it. "That's true."

"I know your name is Janice, and that you're good with medicine, but that's about it."

She raised an eyebrow. "Well, you know more about me than I do you."

Ronan chuckled and gestured for her to follow him away from the whinnying horses and to a soft, light green patch of grass a few feet to the left. She hesitated as he strode away, but then looked over to the group of soldiers coming back from the brook. They would be close enough just in case Ronan tried something.

Janice turned her gaze to the young man who patted the ground next to where he sat.

"Come sit," he called.

He definitely didn't seem threatening. She shrugged to herself and moved to sit next to him.

It was beginning to climb into the early afternoon, but the grass was still wet from the morning dew. Janice didn't mind, however. The dampness of the ground was refreshing after riding in the saddle for an hour.

"Well, I'll start," Ronan said after she sat. "You already know my name, so I'll tell you where I come from. I lived in Greriveth in my childhood, but my father died recently    "

"I'm so sorry!"

He waved her condolences away. "I've long been over it. Anyway— "

"What about your mother?"

Ronan's mouth was half-open from trying to speak before she interrupted him a second time, but at the mention of his mother, his face grew dark.

"She's alive, but she left Father and me a long time ago."

Janice took the new information he gave her about his mother as a cue to not push the subject. Ronan gave a her a side-glance to see if she was about to say more. He smiled to see her mouth closed, and eyes shifted to her feet.

"I lived in Mardasia for a bit. In a little village, and now I'm here."

Janice perked up. "What village?"

"Glenam."

Her shoulders fell, having hoped that he had news of Marviton. "I've never been to Glenam."

"But you've been to Mardasia?"

She nodded. "That's my home."

Ronan cocked his head to the side, it being his turn for curiosity. "Why are you in Polart?"

"Now, that's a *long* story." Janice turned her attention to the grass and began pulling out a few blades with her fingers. "I'm the Polartian Queen's sister."

Ronan's mouth dropped to the floor. "Really? The Queen who was forced to play the Mardasian princess?"

Before Janice could answer, Emmett hollered to the party that they should get on the road once again.

"We're less than an hour away, I believe," the soldier said.

Ronan stood up and stretched his arms high above his head with a yawn, then offered a hand to Janice. She took it and rose herself, then moved to accept Emmett's help back onto the horse.

Once she was astride the saddle, she craned her neck back to watch Ronan take his own seat. She really didn't know much about him, but the few words they shared gave her hope that he was a potential friend.

Janice turned her attention back to the road as Emmett kicked the horse's cream-colored flank and led the group onward. She smiled. It was always nice to make some friends in Polart, especially when such relationships for her were few and far between.

# Chapter 6

Crops were trampled over and taken, houses had broken doors hanging on their hinges, there were many areas and buildings with fire damage... but what sent a pang through Janice's heart the most were the villagers crowding inside of their various homes with looks of fear and pain on their dirt-stained faces. They were in bad shape, and Janice counted at least five injured as they passed the people in Bymead to Lord Warren's manor on the outskirts of the little town.

Janice was surprised to hear a nobleman presided over Bymead— he was almost like a local ruler. The guards told her just before arriving that such things were common in Polart. Mardasia didn't have "ruling lords," but it was a much smaller kingdom. She couldn't imagine what life would have been like with a lord overlooking and running the happenings within her home of Marvition. How strange that would have been.

"This is terrible," Ronan said on his own horse that he rode with one of the soldiers.

The eight horses in their group of eight soldiers, Ronan, and Janice rode slowly and close together within the narrow streets.

"If only I had been here!" he breathed.

Janice flashed a look at the young man. The young man had already proven that he cared for other people— once with helping Helga and her son, and again with wanting to help in Bymead. As she stared at Ronan, the hot sun began to peek from behind the houses and few storefronts and glinted radiantly off his pale hair, almost making it look more gold than a white-blond. She cocked her head. Maybe if he put on a little weight, he could be an okay-looking man.

Ronan shot her a look and grinned. "What?"

Janice blinked twice and turned away. "Just thinking."

His lips twitched as he tried to suppress a laugh. "Of course."

Janice kept her eyes on the road. They hadn't arrived more than five minutes ago, but they were already reaching the edge of Bymead.

"It is a very small town, isn't it?" she said, quietly so the villagers intently watching them pass couldn't hear.

Emmett grunted in agreement behind her. His arms tightened around her. The movement was most likely from an instinctual urge to protect her, but she blushed as his forearms pressed against her waist. She shook her head and tried to keep her focus on the task at hand.

Janice shuddered as she felt like she was being watched. After darting her eyes about for the source of the stares, she met Ronan's gaze once again. He hadn't taken her eyes off her since before. Why was he staring so intently?

"What?"

He flinched, flushing slightly, but then shrugged. "Just thinking."

Janice couldn't repress her chuckles at his rebuttal. "Well played."

He shrugged again, moving his gaze back to the road. "I thought so."

"We're here!" Emmett called to the entire party.

Horses whinnied as they were pulled to a stop. Janice craned her neck up at the building before them.

"Well, this is... impressive," she said.

What she really wanted to say was "gaudy." The gray stone was polished until it glinted blindingly from the sun's rays, and the building stood so tall she had to crane her neck all the way back to see the top. Gold encased the frame of the doorway and lined the three, broad steps leading up to the entrance.

Ronan whistled. "You can say that again."

"It's impressive," Janice repeated.

The young man shot her a look and barked out a laugh. "I like you, Janice."

The entire party dismounted from their horses. Emmett leapt from the horse he shared with Janice first, then helped her down. The feeling of his hands clasped around her waist made her blush. Every horse was handed to three stable boys waiting in front of the entrance. Janice eyed them curiously as they led the horses to the back.

"With Bymead so obviously destitute, this lord seems to have no problem with his own financial stability," Janice grumbled.

"You might find that Lord Warren is actually rather kind and personable."

Janice furrowed her brows at Emmett's defense of Warren. How could a man who was obviously enjoying his riches amongst the chaos of the village he oversaw be a good person?

Just as soon as the group began to climb the steps, the massive doors were heaved open by a sickly thin man with the bushiest black beard Janice had ever seen.

"Sir Emmett, and..." he paused with a deep scowl on his face as he surveyed the group. "And party."

Emmett approached the man and shook his hand firmly. "You must be Lord Warren's steward."

The steward lifted his pointy nose into the air proudly. "That I am, sir. Jasper's my name."

"Pleased to meet you." Emmett clapped Jasper's back enthusiastically, making the thin man grow into a coughing fit.

"Right— right— this way," he said through his coughs.

Emmett followed directly behind the steward, then Janice, then the other guards, then Ronan. Though the doorway was wide, the corridor directly inside narrowed quickly and forced all of them to walk single file.

"It's so dark," Ronan said a little too loudly from

the back of the line.

Jasper shot an annoyed look behind himself. "New candles cost money, and Lord Warren is striving to give all he can to the people of Bymead right now."

Ronan didn't reply, embarrassed by his rude comment, but he was right about the darkness as the group stumbled over each others' heels. Janice was barely able to see the candelabras lining the red-papered walls. There was not a single candle lit. The steward's explanation for the lack of light, however, gave Janice the hope she craved that Emmett was right about Warren's character.

Soon they reached a hallway branching off from the previous one that grew wider, allowing most to walk side by side. The new path also had windows lining its walls, letting in a welcome amount of daylight to the darkness inside. Where the Polartian castle had paintings of crusty, old monarchs adorning their hallways, Janice quite liked the feel of a line of windows spanning across their path.

"Lord Warren is in the dining hall." The steward pointed directly in front of them.

Janice gawked at the double doors that lined up from the floor and all the way to the high ceiling.

"He asked to meet with you alone, Sir Emmett." He eyed the rest of the group with narrowed eyes.

Emmett held his hands up in assurance. "Jasper, everyone in this party is here to help. I'm sure Lord Warren won't mind updating *all* of us."

The steward grunted and with a quick turn on his

heel, strode frustratedly away.

"He's pleasant," Ronan said.

Everyone slowly turned to look at Ronan with eyebrows raised. He took two steps backward.

"Sorry," he whispered.

Emmett shook his head, but let out a slight chuckle. He moved to knock on the pinewood doors, varnished to a deep red. The sound of his knock echoed through the wood as if the doors were hollow.

"Come in!" a strong voice called.

Rolling his shoulders back, Emmett pushed on the doors and strode in. Janice stood frozen for a moment as she watched how confident he looked. It was admirable and quite... well, attractive.

"Miss Wallander?" One of the other soldiers poked her gently in the back.

She shook herself from her gawking as her face grew hot. "Sorry. So sorry."

Taking a deep breath, she shuffled into the room with the rest of the group following directly behind her. They entered what must have been a dining hall, and the steps of their many feet echoed loudly against the stone floor. Janice grimaced at the dirt caked on her boots, not wanting to trample mud all over the manor's polished floors. There was an oval table directly in front of them, spanning the length of the room. The dining hall wasn't nearly as large as the one in the castle, but Janice still found herself finding the size completely unnecessary.

A tall, middle-aged man sat in the middle of the

table, facing the group. His back was pressed against the stained glass window that circled all along the wall. The glass depicted a beautiful woman with golden hair kneeling demurely in front of a rose bush. One hand was bleeding from the thorns of the rose, but the other hand tended to the bush despite her injuries. As Janice stared at the picture, tears sprung to her eyes as she studied the woman. She was similar to what her mother once looked like.

"Welcome!' Warren bellowed, pushing his chair back to stand.

Janice winced as his chair bumped roughly against the stained glass, then sighed in relief to see that the beautiful image remained intact. What a shame it would be for such an intriguing piece to shatter.

"Lord Warren," Emmett said with a bow. He glanced at his companions to follow suit.

Janice scrambled to provide a somewhat graceful curtsy but failed miserably. Warren didn't seem to notice, however. He shared a warm smile with everybody in turn, light blue eyes twinkling kindly.

"I'm so glad the Regent sent so much help."

Janice raised an eyebrow. Lord Warren really *was* kind to ignore the fact that the Regent, in reality, sent so little help.

"I assume Lionel informed you of the bandits that raided Bymead," Warren continued.

"Yes, my lord. We were told bandits raided and were overly aggressive," Emmett replied.

Lord Warren bowed his head sadly. "Yes, many

were injured, and we lost two very young souls."

Janice bit her lip to keep it from trembling, realization dawning on her that she was the acting physician for these poor people. How could she ever be up to the task? How had she even *thought* she could be?

"Do you think they will come back?" Emmett said.

Warren shook his head determinedly. "I don't think so. They were obviously Polartian. Usually, bandits who raid villages within their own kingdoms tend to move on and quickly— in fear of recognition or severe punishment for treasonous behavior."

"How are you financially? Your steward said something about doing all you can to help the villagers' financial well-being."

Lord Warren let out a long breath of air, running tan fingers through his raven hair that glinted with hints of silver. The worry lines drawing into his forehead made him seem ten years older than before.

"We are strapped," he said. "I've distributed nearly everything I could, including food. I also stopped collecting the regular Polartian taxes, I hope the Regent won't mind."

Emmett suppressed a smile. "Well, I can assure you the King and Queen won't mind. Once they return, I am sure you will be greatly rewarded for your efforts."

Warren visibly relaxed. "That's good to hear."

"What are your priorities as far as the help we give first?"

"Do you have a physician with you?"

Emmett gestured to Janice and gave her an encouraging smile. "She is not the court physician, but she has proved to be quite skilled and knowledgeable about medicine."

Lord Warren studied her for a moment. "You look familiar. Have we met?"

Janice gulped nervously, still feeling the pressure of the responsibility on her shoulders. "I don't think so, my lord."

"She is Queen Mildred's sister," Emmett contributed. "They do have some similarities. Maybe that's who you're thinking of."

Warren's face lit up. "Oh, yes! I see it! I can see it in the face."

Janice shifted her feet uncomfortably. She never liked being the center of attention.

He leaned forward with a big smile. "Your sister is a *wonderful* queen. If you are anything like her, I trust you'll provide just what we need."

Janice felt her limbs grow stiff, but she forced a smile. "Thank you, Lord Warren."

"Anything else we can do while Janice tends to the injured?" Emmett said.

Warren began to mindlessly draw circles into the marble of his dining table. "I hate to ask it, but, like I was saying, Bymead's financial stability is incredibly lacking. Is there... well, did the Regent give you anything to help with that?"

Emmett's face fell. "I'm so sorry. But we can help rebuild, tend to gardens and fields—"

"Janice can spin straw into gold!"

# Chapter 7

Janice's eyes grew wide at the outburst. Had she heard that correctly? She wasn't the only person to turn to Ronan standing in the background. His feet were planted strongly, and he nodded violently as he pointed to Janice.

And then all eyes turned to her. Emmett looked her up and down with an incredulous look on his face.

"What are you talking about?" Janice directed to Ronan through gritted teeth. She was starting to regret bringing someone they knew nothing about along. He *had* to be insane.

"What?" he said, holding up his hands defensively. "Magic isn't outlawed in Polart, is it?"

His large eyes pleaded with her to play along. Janice merely folded her arms and stared him down.

"No... it's not..." Emmett said slowly, chewing at the words as if they tasted bitter in his mouth. "But sorcery hasn't made enough of an appearance in Polart to really make such decisions against or for it."

Janice shook her head, appalled by the situation. "I don't know what he's talking about! I can't spin straw into gold!" Her cries were louder than she had intended, and she felt her cheeks burn as each person continued to stare.

"Uh, Janice. Can I talk to you for a second?"

Without waiting for a reply, Ronan turned on his heel and strode out of the dining hall. Janice's jaw dropped to the floor. This was ridiculous! But after studying the frozen expressions of shock on everyone's faces and realizing no one moved to stop her, she sighed and followed after the crazy boy.

She heaved the doors shut behind them, struggling greatly under their weight, but Ronan made no move to help her. Just another point against him.

"Ronan," Janice tried to say calmly, "what on *earth* are you doing?"

He winced at the harshness in her tone, Janice having failed to remain as calm as she wanted to.

"Of course *you* can't spin straw into gold. But I can."

Janice narrowed her eyes and clenched her fists. She was not one to get angry very often, but Ronan was getting on her last nerve.

"Please explain," she spat.

Ronan gulped, stretching out the collar of his tunic. "Is it hot in here?"

Janice began to tap her foot, impatient.

"Okay, okay. I was born with certain... abilities. Things like seeing tiny glimpses of the future through my dreams, reading someone's thoughts—"

Janice gasped and grabbed at her face, feeling violated. "Read thoughts?"

He held up his hands and waved them back and

forth. "It's not what you think! Only one thought here and there, and I have to *really* concentrate."

"Oh, that makes it *so* much better," she said, folding her arms.

"I trained under a skilled warlock for a few years and learned some useful skills. Just a few weeks ago, I was spinning straw into gold in a little town in Mardasia. Only to *help* people, mind you."

Janice cocked her head in curiosity. "Mardasia? What town?"

"Glenarm."

"Oh," she said, disappointed. She was hoping to maybe hear some news of Marviton.

"Anyway," he continued, "a witch—a very powerful, famous witch among my type of folk— warned me to stop doing it. I want to help these people in Bymead so I thought saying you could spin straw into gold was a better idea than getting caught by the witch again..."

Janice didn't know what to think. She started pacing the width of the corridor, wearing the rug beneath her feet. Magic was not heard of in Mardasia, but it was— apparently— becoming more and more prominent in Polart. A year or two ago, she might have laughed and scoffed at this young man, but now, especially after the mysterious stories Milly had told her, she found herself believing him.

"Did you think about the fact that this 'witch' might get me in trouble instead of you?"

Ronan grimaced. "No, I didn't think of that."

Janice threw her arms up into the air, exasperated. "You can't be blurting stuff like that out to a room full of strong and powerful people, Ronan! Actually, you shouldn't to anyone."

"It's not against the law," he huffed.

Janice pressed her back against the bare wall next to the dining hall's doors and slid to the floor. A headache was beginning to grind in her temples. Ronan shuffled over and sat next to her.

"Please, Janice? Just play along for a day or two. I think it can really help these people."

Janice banged her head against the wall, knowing what she was about to say might make her just as insane as Ronan.

"Fine. Only because *you* got us into this mess, and I expect you to get us out of it. And I will only 'spin straw into gold' if Lord Warren wants me to, which I highly doubt."

# *Chapter 8*

Janice stood abruptly and marched to the double doors, pushing them open with all the strength she could muster. She strode into the room and without making eye contact with any person, began to speak:

"Yes, I can spin straw into gold. I was too scared to admit it before, but— with your permission, of course, Lord Warren— I am willing to spin some for the people of Bymead."

Out of the corner of her eye, Janice saw Ronan silently applauding her and mouthing the words "thank you."

Nothing but silence met her ears. She dared a look at Emmett, but he seemed impressed by the way she presented the proposal. She was surprised by it, herself. Janice had never been good at confrontation in any form, and now she was confronting a small crowd *and* lying to them. She bit her lip. She didn't like it one bit.

Lord Warren was frozen before the table, gawking at her. "Uh, I don't know what to say."

Janice felt her legs begin to wobble, but she forced herself to stand firm.

"Just *making* money might cause some trouble," Emmett said.

Janice flushed. She felt overwhelmingly embarrassed by the situation Ronan had put her in. Emmett was right: she didn't know enough about economics, but a random addition of gold might throw things into a bit of disarray. Not to mention the inevitably of greedy people asking her— Ronan, really — for more than they needed.

"Maybe if Miss Wallander spun a single, set amount here in my home, and we distribute *just* that much, it won't be too much of an issue." Warren's eyes pleaded with the entire group. "Like I said, we're really desperate."

Emmett frowned. "I don't know if I like it."

"If I may interject, Lord Warren is the highest-ranked in here." Ronan cleared his throat. "I mean, it's his decision."

Lord Warren sat back down in his chair and rubbed his face with his hands. Every person in the room watched him. Janice held her breath, not sure what she hoped his answer to be.

"I say we try it," he finally said. "Just a little bit. Make sure the people have enough for some food and supplies until the King and Queen return and can send more money."

Emmett's frown grew deeper, but he stood up straight and saluted, the other soldiers following suit. "As you wish, my lord."

"Janice, if you would go treat who you can medicinally first, then come back before nightfall. I will have a spinning wheel prepared for you."

She gave a small curtsy. At Warren's dismissal, she scurried away and back out to the village quicker than any of her companions. She didn't want to face any of the questions and stares. Especially from Emmett. Any chance she might have had with him was long gone— not that she was expecting it much, anyway. But now Janice felt she had also lost his respect. Though magic was more common in Polart, most people still didn't know how to think of it, and her supposed concealment of her abilities did not help at all.

She muttered under her breath as she walked along the cobbled path to the first house. The next time she was alone with Ronan, she would give him a piece of her mind.

The first few doors had no immediate need for her, but the fifth house directed her to the end of the village, where she would find the most injuries. The walk from one end of Bymead to the other was not long or difficult, but the sight of mourning people and destroyed homes was what made the walk grueling. Janice had a hard time with the suffering of others. If she could snap her fingers and make everything better, she would in a heartbeat.

She halted in the middle of the street. A few passersby bumped into her because of the abruptness of her stop. With shock, she realized that "spinning straw into gold" with Ronan was a weird, twisted way of snapping her fingers and making everything better. Even if every family was given a little bit, they could eat for weeks until Milly returned home with Alexander. And once they came back, they would— without a doubt— show immense generosity to the people of Bymead. She just needed to help them make it until then.

Janice rolled her shoulders back and let out a long breath of air. She continued on her walk in search of patients, feeling slightly more encouraged than before.

# Chapter 9

Janice and Ronan followed Lord Warren down the winding corridors that led deep within his manor. Only a few candles scattered throughout the building provided what light they had to see the path before them, reminding Janice of Warren's attempts to save money, but Lord Warren knew his home well enough to navigate the hallways without any problems.

After a few hours in the town treating a variety of wounds ranging from all levels of severity, Janice received a message from one of Lord Warren's servants requesting her presence once again. Emmett had asked her if she'd like company. Everything in her wanted to say yes and to have the handsome guard at her side in a precarious situation, but it would have defeated the purpose of Ronan's and her — well, more Ronan's— plan. She refused his offer as politely as she could, explaining that Ronan knew how to help her with the spinning.

"How *did* Ronan know you could spin straw into gold?" Emmett had asked suspiciously. "You two just met."

Ronan had been eavesdropping on their conversation at that moment and chimed in, "When we stopped to rest the horses on the way here, Janice and I got to talking, and I remembered seeing her in Mardasia *years* ago— when we were merely teenagers. I caught her spinning gold once then. That type of thing is hard to forget."

Emmett had seemed reluctant to accept the tale but had asked no further questions, most likely assuming it would do no good. Janice replayed the conversation over and over again in her head as she and Ronan followed the nobleman. What would she do when Emmett and the others reported to the Regent about her "abilities?" There was no way she could keep up the farce forever. She would just have to get Ronan to tell the truth before then. Maybe they could do it in a way the scary witch he never stopped reminding her about wouldn't figure out.

Janice, Lord Warren, and Ronan finally reached a secluded corner with a little wooden door tucked away in the darkness. It seemed rather ominous to Janice, but she didn't ask any questions.

"One of my maids set up a workspace for you here."

Lord Warren didn't even have to turn the knob to open the aging door. It creaked loudly and revealed a dungeon-like room with dull, gray stone for its floors and walls. There were no windows in sight, and the only light in the room glinted from a single stub of a candle beside an old spinning wheel. Next to it on the other side, far enough away from the candle's flame so as not to start a fire, was a small pile of straw. Janice crinkled her nose at the musty smell emanating around her.

"So, we only want a meager amount of gold to distribute to each family. Do you think that much will do?" Lord Warren asked, referring to the straw.

Janice gave a side glance to Ronan, and he gave her a subtle nod.

"That should be fine," she said.

"Good, good." Warren eyed Ronan next to her. "And you need his help?"

"Yes. I need some help feeding the wheel when I'm handling so much gold on the end," she said, reciting what Ronan had told her to say.

Lord Warren nodded, then began shifting his feet uncomfortably. "Uh, can I watch?"

"No!" she cried.

He raised an eyebrow at her.

"It's just— just..." She scrambled for an excuse, but Ronan saved her.

"She doesn't work well under a lot of pressure," he said. "Having me in here is already pushing it a bit."

Janice stiffened, waiting for Warren's reply, but he merely shrugged.

"I'll leave you to it, then. How long will it take you?"

She thought back to what Ronan had told her to say: "Until morning."

Janice and Ronan watched as Warren left the room and shut the door behind himself, making the room seem even darker than it had before. Just as soon as the door clicked shut, Ronan cracked his knuckles and moved over to the wheel.

"I'd better get to work," he said.

# Chapter 10

Watching Ronan was like watching a master at his craft. The way his strong hands moved as the wheel spun, with an elegant dexterity, was mesmerizing. Janice sat huddled in the corner as he fed one tiny bundle after another into the wheel and spun it. He chanted a group of words each time, words she couldn't understand. His eyes were closed, and he seemed to be in his own world.

The first bit of gold began to clink on the stone floor in the form of a thick, shining thread. As Ronan spun faster and faster, the spool slowly began to grow.

"I didn't think you could actually do it," she breathed, feeling more in awe than frightened by his abilities. It was incredible.

Ronan didn't seem to hear her. His body trembled from his spells as he continued to mutter the strange words. The candle beside the wheel flickered against a wind she couldn't feel. After another two minutes, or so, Ronan's hands slowed, and the wheel shuddered to a halt. He slumped over in the stool he sat on and fell to the floor in a heap.

"Ronan!" Janice cried, rushing over to his side.

"Are you alright?" She wrapped her arms underneath his chest and grunted under the attempt to lift him from the dusty floor.

His pale, blue eyes fluttered open, and he groaned. "What happened?"

"You were spinning the straw, and then you fainted!"

"Not again." He placed a palm on his forehead.

Janice pursed her lips. "Again? This has happened before?"

"Turning something into a completely different object— *especially* into gold— is one of the most tiring spells to do. It's draining."

His body relaxed even more in her grip from the exhaustion. Her arms shook under his weight, so, as gently as her little strength could muster, she set him down on the floor face-up. Ronan craned his neck to look at the straw he still hadn't spun, grunting from the effort.

"I need to finish."

Janice hushed him, placing a finger on his lips. "No. You need to rest."

He closed his eyes in defeat. "I'll rest, but I'm only a third of the way done. Wake me in no less than an hour."

Janice felt as if she had no choice but to accept that and scooted away from him. She moved back to her corner and stared at him, feeling worry lines drawing in between her brows. Seeing Ronan collapse had scared her, and she didn't want this pointless endeavor to *kill* him!

She stared at him for a few minutes more, trying to force her tired eyes to stay open. But soon, sleep became too strong and overtook her.

"Janice. Janice!"

Ronan roughly shook at her shoulder until she slowly began to wake up. She felt groggy as she moved into a sitting position from where she lay on the floor. Janice looked around herself, studying the darkness and forgetting where she was and what she was doing. She looked up at Ronan's face, barely even able to see his eyes glaring down at her from the dark. Then, realization dawned on her.

"Oh."

"Why didn't you wake me up! Who *knows* how long it has been?"

Janice yawned. "I'm sorry. I was so tired."

"Look." She couldn't really see it, but she sensed his movement pointing in the direction of the spinning wheel. "The candle burned out. We have no light. I can't finish!"

Just as soon as Ronan finished speaking, the door creaked open, and Lord Warren peeked his head in.

"It really is dark in here," he said, stumbling towards them through the darkness, but even the light from the hallway seeping in through the open door was enough to make Janice squint uncomfortably. "I'm sorry about that."

"Why did you put us in such a crummy place with no windows, Lord Warren?" Ronan growled. He was obviously still very exhausted.

Warren blinked twice at the remark but chose not to reply. He squinted at the gold at the foot of the spinning wheel and gasped.

"You actually did it, Janice!"

Lord Warren rushed over to the pile of gold. Grunting, he lifted some of the shining, string-like metal and held it close to his eyes.

"It's real," he whispered.

"Of course it is," Ronan grumbled.

Ignoring the grumpy young man once again, Lord Warren glanced at the remaining pile of straw and frowned.

"Why didn't you finish?"

"I can finish tonight," Janice said, thinking quickly. "It's a very tiring spell. What I finished, however, should be a good start.

Warren nodded vehemently. "Yes, it is a *very* good start."

# Chapter 11

The people were beyond grateful. Many mothers and fathers were in tears, and little children danced around the bits of gold they received. Janice had to admit to herself that she was pleased to see the joy among those who really needed some good fortune after the terrible events of the bandit raid.

It didn't go past her how pleased Ronan seemed to be. He nearly choked up many times when helping her, and the Polartian guards distribute the money. The fact that he wasn't getting any credit but was so happy to help the poor people proved to Janice that he really was using his powers for the greater good.

Janice, however, received a mountain of praises, and it made her feel uncomfortable. She hated the attention, not to mention how lying made her feel like each time she accepted the praise with false smiles. Even Emmett had warmed up to the supposed powers, often providing her with compliments and even admiration. In other circumstances, she might have welcomed such attention from the handsome soldier, but it was all based on falsehoods. She wished more than anything that she could tell the truth and direct all the credit to

Ronan.

It took all the way through the morning and late afternoon to distribute the gold, and until Janice found a moment to eat something and catch a quick nap before another night of watching Ronan spin straw.

Lord Warren was letting Janice and the others stay in some of his extra rooms during their stay, and she was grateful to have a chamber to herself, being the only girl in the party. Janice attempted to navigate the dark corridors of the manor on her own, trying to find the room the steward had shown her the day before.

She had only seen the room once, having spent the night in the workroom with Ronan and a pile of straw, so she got lost quickly. Janice stopped in the fifth hallway she had decided to try looking down and rubbed her face with her hands. All of a sudden, she heard the faint whispering of voices coming from the end of the corridor. Relieved, she picked up her pace and followed the sound.

After a sharp turn to the left, she saw a stream of yellow light spilling from a half-open door and grinned. The voices were close enough now that she could determine one of them to belong to Lord Warren. She stepped up closer to the door and was about to knock, but was interrupted by the second voice, a low, gruff one, speaking:

"She spins straw into *gold*? You've got to be joking!"

"I am dead serious. We just finished giving some

to the people," Lord Warren replied.

"And you can give some to us, right?"

Janice took in a sharp breath and side-stepped away from the door so as not to be seen. Who was Warren talking to?

She heard the lord chuckle. "I can do better than that. Are you and the other men free tomorrow?"

Janice closed her eyes and leaned in closer to better hear the conversation, but the sound of soft footsteps to her left made her eyes fly open once again.

"What are you doing?"

Janice jumped as Ronan snuck up on her and poked her in the shoulder. She sighed in relief to see it was only him and frantically put a finger up to her lips.

Ronan raised an eyebrow. "Why do I need to be quiet?"

The door beside them was slowly pushed the rest of the way open, and Lord Warren poked his head out. His eyes widened in shock to see Janice and Ronan standing there, and Janice thought she saw a moment of fear flash across his face, but it was gone just as quickly as it had come.

Lord Warren recomposed himself, slipped through the door, and shut it behind himself. Janice's shoulders fell as she wasn't able to catch a glimpse of the man he had been talking to.

"Can I help you two with something?"

Janice wrung her hands together and opened and closed her mouth to say something, but words wouldn't present themselves. The little piece of the conversation she heard between Lord Warren and the stranger sounded more than suspicious, and she didn't know how the lord would react when learning of her attempt to eavesdrop.

"I—I was lost," she finally said.

"Me too!" Ronan chimed in. "And then I found her here. She was just about to knock and ask for your help before I came along."

Janice shot the young man a grateful look, and Lord Warren beamed at the two of them with his arms outstretched welcomingly.

"Of course! Anything I can do to help. Where were you two headed?"

Janice relaxed her tense limbs and smiled back. He didn't seem to have suspected her of listening in on a secret conversation. And even if he did, he appeared too nonchalant and friendly to have been talking about something suspicious. Maybe Janice had been worrying about nothing.

After having rested in the warm, cozy guest room of hers for two hours, Janice had been directed to the workroom for another night of silently watching Ronan spin straw.

She found herself thinking back to the conversation she had overheard in the afternoon. She couldn't dare to believe Lord Warren was up to something, but what could he have meant when he said he could "do better" than give gold to the man he spoke with?

Janice was so deep in her thoughts that the sound of Ronan falling to the floor made her jump in fright.

"Ronan!" she cried, racing to his side as she had the night before. The sight of him fainting was still not a fun thing for her to see, even if she did know the reason for it.

His breathing was ragged, and his eyes opened and closed with a flurry of movement.

"I'm... I'm... I'm okay." His voice quavered against his heavy breathing.

Janice helped him to a sitting position and pointed to where the pile of straw had once been. "You finished it, Ronan. You're done."

The bits of candlelight in the corner of the room revealed a hint of a smile forming on his pale lips. Lord Warren, due to the new availability to some money, put two new candlesticks in the room for them along with a tinderbox to relight them, if needed.

"Thank goodness."

The overwhelming relief in his voice sent a pang through Janice's heart. Ronan was doing so much for these people. He looked even thinner than when she had first met him, and the angles of his cheeks were sinking into deep, worrisome shadows.

"Is there anything I can help you with, or get you? Water, perhaps?"

He shook his head and groaned at the effort it took. "No. Just talk to me. I'm bored."

Her shoulders shook from laughter, not having expected that answer. "You're bored?"

"Yes. *Deathly* bored."

Janice's laughter grew even more, and she snorted. Ronan's eyes grew wide, and he guffawed at the sound she made, causing him to throw himself into a coughing fit.

"What's so funny?" she demanded but still unable to stop her own giggling and snorting.

"Your laugh!" he tried to exclaim through his coughing. "It's so adorable!"

She pushed on his shoulder gently. "Whatever."

Tears were streaming down Ronan's eyes both from the laughter and the coughing. "It's true. I've never heard anything like it."

She flushed a little and averted her gaze to the floor.

"Okay, okay." His voice was hoarse, but he continued: "Tell me something you've never told anyone before."

Janice raised an eyebrow. "Is that going to help your boredom?"

"Oh, immensely."

She chewed at the inside of her cheek, thinking back to something she could say to satiate his odd question.

"I hate living in the castle."

He narrowed his eyes at her answer. "No one would hate living in a castle."

She merely shrugged in reply.

"Okay, answer me this." He sat up straighter before continuing, the color beginning to return to his cheeks. "Why do you hate it so much?"

"I feel like I don't belong. I'm not noble, but I'm the Queen's sister. No one knows how to treat me. And I also miss my simple life in Mardasia. It was actually more... laid back. I miss my garden, my friends..."

Ronan whistled. "You've thought a lot about this, huh?"

She nodded solemnly. "I am *so* happy for Milly, though—"

"Who?"

"The Queen."

"Oh." He waved his hand for her to continue.

"Her husband is so wonderful to her, and she loves being of help to the Polartian people, but I feel completely useless and like I'm just... there."

Ronan stroked his chin as he thought. "Why don't you just leave?"

Her eyes widened, and she shook her head violently. "I can't be apart from my sister— not again!"

"Queen Mildred is the one who was kidnapped and forced to play the Mardasian Princesses, right?"

Janice's stomach churned at the memory. But, if it hadn't happened, Milly wouldn't have found her true love.

"Yeah, she was."

"You know what, how about I tell you a secret of mine," Ronan said, trying to cheer her up. "My real name isn't Ronan."

Janice perked up and leaned forward. "What do you mean?"

He darted his eyes about the room as if someone were listening. "I don't want *anyone* else to know, okay?"

She held up her hands in promise, enormously curious to know the reasoning for such secrecy. Ronan shifted where he sat, trousers scraping loudly against the stone.

"Are you going to tell me?" Janice pressed.

"I'm getting to it!" He closed his eyes and took a deep breath. "My real name is Rumpelstiltskin."

"Rumpelstiltskin?" Janice threw head back and shook with laughter, tears streaming down her face. "You've got to be joking! What type of name is that?"

Ronan's— no, *Rumpelstiltkin's* face had darkened with a deep scowl pressed into his jaw. "It's not funny."

"Oh, it's more than just funny." Janice wiped at the tears under her eyes. "It's hilarious."

He grumbled under his breath at her inability to stop laughing, but then she snorted, causing Rumpelstiltskin's lips to twitch into a tiny smile.

"Not as hilarious as your laugh."

"Hey, you said it was cute!"

He shrugged. "I changed my mind. It's more funny than cute."

Janice quickly tried to change the subject back to his peculiar name: "What made your parents call you 'Rumpelstiltskin' of all names?"

He sat up on his knees enthusiastically, seemingly feeling better from the draining spell.

"Okay, now that's a *great* story."

Janice shifted forward with her palms resting on the cold floor in front of her, eager to hear this "great story." After what seemed to be too long of a pause, she leaned away with a frown on her face.

"Are you going to tell me?"

"Nope."

She scoffed at Ronan but reached over and playfully pushed at his chest. "You're insufferable!"

"That's why you like me!" He flashed her a cheeky grin, and she couldn't help but laugh at his ridiculousness.

"Should I start calling you Rumpelstiltskin now?"

His eyes grew wide in horror. "Please don't."

All of a sudden, the door behind them burst open, and Emmett, with a shining sword brandished protectively, ran through with Lord Warren right on his heels.

"Janice! Ronan!" Emmett placed his hands on his knees, sword still in hand, to catch a breath. "They're back. The bandits!"

# Chapter 12

"How many wounded?" Janice cried over the wind as she, Emmett, Lord Warren, and Ronan ran out of the manor and onto the streets. It was still dark outside, and there were a few hours left until dawn. The area directly by Warren's home wasn't where the raiding was happening, but she could hear the cries and shouts not far from where they were.

"About four people, but that was before I left!" Emmett yelled back to her.

Ronan was stumbling behind the rest of the group, crying out in pain as he tried to catch up. He was still recovering from his spell. Janice slowed to help him, but he waved her away.

"Go! You need to help the people. I'll come as soon as I can."

Emmett and Lord Warren hadn't noticed the delay and were already making significant distance ahead of her. She glanced back at Ronan and squeezed his arm.

"Will you be alright?"

He nodded and pushed at her side. "Just go!"

Janice threw herself back into a sprint to catch

up with the two men. They had finally noticed her absence and slowed until she reached them once more. Emmett flashed a worried look back at Ronan.

"Is he not coming?"

"An old wound is flaring up," she lied. "He'll try to catch up later."

Once they made it to where the chaos was happening, at the very center of the town, Janice gasped at the sight of the villagers screaming in fear as a group of about a dozen men tore into their homes and grabbed what little they could find. Fathers threw themselves in front of their families and homes, but only to be brutally kicked or cut down and out of the way. Emmett's soldiers were doing their best to stop the chaos, but they were succeeding very little.

One ruffian barreled out of a home before it toppled to the ground from flames with a long string of gold in his hand.

"I found some of it!" he cried.

His comrades cheered, urging each other to find more. How had the bandits learned of the magical gold?

Janice's feet couldn't move as she watched the terrible scene unfold. Her eyes darted about herself in a frenzy, and she counted eight people on the ground screaming in pain from deep cuts or heavy punches— some were even unconscious from blood loss, and two of the victims were children...

Blood pounded loudly in her ears as her vision

began to grow dark, and she barely heard Emmett calling out her name until he grabbed her shoulders and shook her. It was rough but necessary.

"Janice," he said, intently searching her eyes for a response. The starting of flames as the bandits cast torches onto the homes surrounding them cast shadows into the line of his jaw. "These people need your help. I'll help you move the wounded somewhere safer."

Her bottom lip trembled, but she nodded determinedly. Emmett rushed over to one of the injured villagers and moved him away from the chaos. Janice followed the soldier to the empty home and gestured for the victim to be placed on the wooden dining table directly inside. Emmett did so, then ran out to retrieve more wounded.

Janice approached the modest table and set her physician's bag next to the moaning man, wincing as the table's legs began wobbling precariously. The last thing she needed was a patient falling through and getting a concussion. After it stopped moving, she carefully moved her hands to the tear in the man's pant leg and grimaced at the deep cut in his thigh. He was losing a lot of blood and quickly.

Forcing her body to stop trembling, she gave the man an encouraging smile. "My name's Janice."

His wrinkled hand grabbed at her arm, and his brown eyes widened in recognition. "You're the gold lady."

She grimaced at the nickname but nodded anyway. "That's one thing I'm known for. But I'm also going to help your leg."

Janice rummaged through the bag for something to staunch the blood, but he grabbed her again.

"Are you going to heal me with magic? People are saying that's how you got the gold... you made it. Out of *straw*." The man started retching and relaxed his grip on her.

Janice moved faster with treating his wound. "Sir, please stop talking. I need to stop the bleeding."

By the time she finished all she could for the first victim, Emmett had brought in about five more.

"I'll... I'll keep bringing them in," he stammered through his heavy breathing. "I'm also trying to fight and protect wherever I can."

Janice nodded and quickly moved to her next patients, two little boys clasping each other's hands in fear. They were both blond with bits of black speckled about the locks like dashes of pepper. The shared uniqueness of such a trait made her assume the two were brothers.

She ran her fingers over their arms, studying their cuts and bruises. Luckily, they were just surface wounds. Nothing a bit of cleaning, and a touch of love couldn't fix.

"You're the witch," the taller one whispered. He couldn't have been more than eight, the other maybe five or six.

Janice pursed her lips. She didn't want to be known as "the witch," especially when she was treating the victims with traditional medicine.

After an hour of treating the patients Emmett

had brought in to her, she collapsed on the floor by the hearth. The coals inside were still a bit warm from the fire that most likely was burning right before the bandits made their appearance.

The moaning and wailings of the victims in the room started to die down after she treated each of them, most even falling asleep. Janice rested her face in her knees and felt a wave of exhaustion rush over her. It took her a few moments to realize she couldn't hear the screaming of the villagers and the cruel laughter of the bandits. She lifted her head up in confusion, trying to focus on listening for the distant chaos, but it was gone. Then she realized that Emmett hadn't returned with more wounded in a while… What was going on?

As if summoned by her thoughts, the wooden door burst open from a kick of a round, burly man. It splintered and began to hang halfway off its hinges from the hit. Janice leapt from the floor, and the others in the house with her jolted from the sound.

The bandit grinned underneath his thick, black beard, flashing a row of yellow teeth. He then scanned the group of injured in front of him.

"The sick house," he said. "We were wondering where the injured were disappearing off to." He moved his black eyes to Janice, who was inching away into the corner. "You must be the healer. I'll take care of you first."

Janice froze for a split second as he spoke. She felt like she had heard his voice somewhere before, but she couldn't quite put her finger on it.

The man shifted the club in his grip and started to rush at her. It felt like it was happening in slow motion as Janice held her breath and squinted her eyes shut.

"No!" someone shouted.

Janice's eyes flew open to see who the voice belonged to. Lord Warren stood in the doorway with his arms raised to the bandit.

"Not that one," he said. "She's the spinner."

# Chapter 13

After calling in a few other bandits, Lord Warren ordered them to drag Janice, along with the wounded in the house with her, to the middle of town. The victims who could barely walk stumbled to the ground as they were prodded by the men. Every time Janice moved to help them, the bearded bandit with the intimidating club— the one she now knew as the man Lord Warren was speaking to when she was eavesdropping on him—tightened his grip around her waist and urged her onward as Lord Warren ordered his men to leave the weakest behind and in the middle of the street.

Janice bore her eyes into the back of Warren, cursing him under her breath. While she watched him stroll ahead, everything was starting to make sense: he probably aided in the first bandit attack, taking the people's money for himself, pretending to look financially unstable to the royal party to keep up his farce. Then, once she gave the people some magical gold, another reason to raid arose itself.

She chided herself for not telling Emmett or anyone else about his secret conversation from the day before, but she had to admit that she was shocked, having been under the impression that Lord Warren was a kind, compassionate man. Yes, she was shocked, but she was mostly angry. He was *not* a good man, he was greedy and selfish. He walked ahead of the group with his arms clasped behind him, and broad shoulders rolled back confidently, nose turned up into the air. It took everything in her not to tear herself free from her captor and claw at the traitor until he bled.

Was he the bandit leader? It definitely seemed like it as the ruffians listened to everything he told them to do. Janice shook her head. How terrible to take advantage of the village one oversaw and attack it. Twice!

Janice clenched her fists and mindlessly dug her dirty nails into the bandit's arm. He cried out and pried her hands away.

"Don't you go tryin' anything!" the bandit hissed in her ear. Her eyes burned at the smell of alcohol on his breath.

Once they made it to their destination, Janice felt like she might be sick. There were about a dozen more injured in the area, and almost no building that wasn't burning. Janice gazed around the street with tears biting at her eyes. The remaining villagers not injured or missing sat in a line in the middle of the street. Parents were holding their screaming children, the elderly were rocking back and forth from coughing fits, and soot from the fires covered each person's face and clothes. The villagers were being watched intently by the remaining bandits in

Lord Warren's party, threatening looks daring anyone to try running.

Janice darted her eyes to each person's face nervously, counting all the royal guards except one: Emmett. A claw of fear grabbed around her heart as she looked over the people again and confirmed his absence. She also couldn't find Ronan, but she felt an inkling of hope that he was able to get away from the chaos before it was too late.

Janice was tossed roughly in front of the line of people. Her hands scraped uncomfortably against the stone of the street. She felt the fabric of her dress tear at the knees as she slid across the ground. One by one, the rest from the sick house— the ones who actually made it— were thrown alongside her.

Lord Warren clicked his tongue. "Boys, boys. No need to be so rough." He paced in front of the terrified group, face stoic and unreadable. He stopped his pacing in front of Janice and squatted down to her level. "In my defense, I told them not to get as out of hand as they did. It was unnecessary to burn down buildings and hurt so many people."

Without even thinking, Janice spat into Warren's face. He didn't even flinch as the spittle hit his eye and wiped it away with a chuckle.

"I didn't take you for the feisty type."

"I didn't take you for the criminal type," she growled back.

Lord Warren threw his head back and laughed. Janice narrowed her eyes at him. It seemed that everybody had misjudged his character, including

Emmett. Her eyes widened at the thought of the missing soldier.

"Where's Emmet?"

"Ah, now that was a necessary loss."

"What are you talking about?" Janice held herself back from grabbing the man by his shoulders. Her entire body started shaking, and she bit the inside of her cheek— hard.

Lord Warren interlocked his fingers and stared at Janice, waiting for her to calm down. The flames of the fires surrounding them danced in his blue eyes. They sparkled at her like when they first met, but not with the kindness she had first assumed— with a morbid amusement to the suffering around him.

"Emmett was causing some… issues. Baron there killed him." He waved over to the bearded man with the club. He raised up his weapon with a look of glee plastered on his ugly face.

Janice's limbs suddenly went completely numb, and a bitter taste in the back of her mouth came up that she couldn't seem to get rid of.

"Wh—wh—" she couldn't get the words out, too horrified for her tongue to work correctly. Lord Warren couldn't have killed Emmett, could he? No, it wasn't possible!

"Now, Janice." He leaned closer to her. "We're keeping you alive and well for a very specific reason. I bet you can guess what that reason is."

She still couldn't bring herself to speak. This man killed Emmett. And who knew who else would die by his hand, or even from wounds incurred in the attack?

Lord Warren answered for her: "We need some more of your special gold."

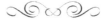

Janice paced back and forth in her prison, the room she had been in many times before to watch Ronan spin straw into gold, but her perspective of waiting around in it was completely different than before. It had never been a *comfortable* space to begin with, but now she truly was a prisoner. Lord Warren had even locked her in, and she couldn't remember him doing that before.

She moved to the door and wiggled at it. It was very old, and with great effort, she might be able to crack through, but Warren most likely set up a group of men to watch the room and make sure she didn't escape.

Janice screamed at the top of her lungs and slammed her fists against the door. It wobbled precariously, but then stilled once again. Moving back to the spinning wheel, she stared at the numerous piles of straw surrounding it. There were about a dozen stacks, all towering high to the ceiling. She had been instructed to spin it all before the next day, or she would be made an example in front of the villagers. Meaning, she assumed, she would be executed. And of course, spinning straw into gold was impossible without Ronan.

As if summoned by her thoughts of him, Janice heard the soft whisper of Ronan's voice echoing around the room and bouncing off the walls to her ears.

"Psst... Janice."

Janice leapt up quickly and ran in circles looking for him. She weaved through the piles of straw, hoping to find him sitting behind one.

"Where are you?"

"Behind you."

She whirled around and saw his head— just his head peeking *through* the stone wall leading to the outside. She put her hand over her mouth to stifle a scream.

"How?" she squeaked.

Ronan slipped the rest of the way through as if he were a ghost, and solid objects were barely an obstacle.

"Are you really going to ask me how? I'm a warlock, remember? We have more important things to discuss."

It took her a moment, but she finally nodded in agreement. Then, she rushed into Ronan's arms and sobbed against his chest. Ronan hesitated a moment but soon wrapped his arms around her and stroked her disheveled hair.

"It was terrible. Lord Warren—" she whispered.

"I know. I saw."

Janice pushed against his chest to look up into his

face, barely illuminated by the small flame dancing on the pathetic candle the bandits gave her to work by.

"Where were you? How much did you see?"

He held up a finger to her lips to stop the questions. "I saw a lot of the aftermath, and I didn't make it on time to help in any way. I stayed hidden in the hopes that I could find an opportunity to do *something*, but once he gathered up some of the villagers, he... he ordered someone to kill Emmett."

Janice gulped, and her lip began to tremble. "How — how did he die?" she stammered.

Ronan shook his head violently and pressed her back into his arms. "You don't wanna know."

Janice whimpered and soaked his shirt with her tears. He smelled strongly of smoke from the fires, which made her eyes water even more.

After a few more moments of listening to her sobs, Ronan gently pulled away.

"Janice, we need to go get help. You're the Queen's sister, right? Maybe you can get her to send more soldiers or something!"

Janice bit her lip. That was true. Milly and her husband had been on their trip for a few weeks now. It was very possible they were home. And if not, there was no way the Regent could say no to such a dire need.

"I definitely think we could get help," she said.

Ronan nodded emphatically, blond bangs bouncing on and off his forehead.

"But I can't go with you."

"What do you mean?" he pressed.

"You need to go alone. But first, I need you to spin this straw."

His jaw dropped to the floor, and he stood frozen. "Uh," he chuckled nervously, "are you joking?"

She shook her head and grabbed his hands. "Ronan, if I don't stay, and if this straw doesn't get spun, Lord Warren and his ruffians might take it out on the people. Families, Ronan! Children and elders who can't even fend for themselves!"

Ronan rubbed his temples and looked as if he were about to cry. "Okay. How long do we have?"

"Well, it's about noon now, right? We have until tomorrow morning."

"That's less than twenty-four hours!"

Janice squeezed his hands and gave him an encouraging smile. "I wouldn't ask this of you if I didn't think it was completely necessary. I *know* it's a draining spell, but I believe in you."

# Chapter 14

Janice felt as if she held Ronan in her arms more through the rest of the day and that night than he was even able to spin. Remarkably, it seemed the young man was getting even thinner each time he attempted the spell for an hour or two, then collapsed in her waiting arms. She knew now not to sit far away from him as he spun, in fear of him falling and cracking his skull open.

Ronan had been pushing himself for days now, and looking at his pale skin, and the hair plastered to his forehead from sweat worried Janice more than she could explain. She had grown to care for Ronan, enjoying his company, sharing laughs, getting to know who he was— a compassionate man who worried more for the people around him than for himself. And his consistent spinning only *proved* those endearing qualities.

Not another half hour went by since Ronan's last fainting spell before he shook himself awake and pushed away from Janice's grip.

"What time is it?" he croaked, nearly careening over. Janice threw her arms out to catch him, but he waved her away.

"I really don't know. You've been spinning for a while, though."

"I need to finish." He pointed to the final pile directly behind him. He had completed nearly half of it. "I think I can do the rest with one more go."

Janice furrowed her brows together and placed a hand on his trembling arm. "Are you sure?"

"Yes."

She watched in admiration as Ronan rose, clenching his jaw with determination, and stepped back over to the spinning wheel. Janice inched closer to the stool he sat on, just in case. Though it seemed impossible, even more color drained from his face as he threw his head back and began chanting the words Janice had grown familiarized to.

"Ment maleas... Ment maleas..."

The chanting went on for a good while, but watching the magic Ronan performed always put Janice into a trance. The more she saw him do it, the more beautiful the spell was. Then, all of a sudden, he stopped mid-spin. His eyes flew open, and he raised a finger to his lips to quiet Janice.

"What is it?" she whispered.

He shook his head violently and gestured for her to stay quiet once more. And then she heard it: voices. They were muffled and too far away to distinguish, but they were definitely coming their way.

"You have to go!" Janice squeaked, grabbing his arms and dragging him off the stool.

"But the straw," he hissed. "I haven't finished!"

"We'll both be killed if they find you here! I'll take

my chances."

Janice pushed him towards the wall she'd watched him *step* through just hours before, but Ronan gripped her arms and stared at her so intensely, she caught her breath. She gazed back into his blue eyes, seeming more crystal than pale and bland when she first met him. With one quick motion, his hands moved up to her face and, before she could even blink, he pressed his lips hard against hers.

For one brief moment, she forgot everything happening around her and melted into Ronan's arms, but that didn't last long. Janice's eyes flew open, and she pulled away quickly.

"You need to go," she whispered, confused and shocked by the kiss.

Without making eye contact with her, Ronan flushed and scurried to the wall. He pulled something out from his pocket, but it was too dark for Janice to see what it was as he popped the small object into his mouth, then, seconds later, stepped through the wall as he had before.

After he left, Janice had a hard time thinking and worrying about the impending arrival of the bandits and Lord Warren because of the feeling of the kiss still lingering on her lips. She brought her fingers up to her mouth as she stared at the wall Ronan disappeared through. It had been unexpected, confusing, but, even though it was for a short moment, she had kissed him back.

Even as the ruffians unlocked and kicked open

the door behind her, that's what remained on her mind.

"I'm surprised, Janice. I didn't actually expect you to do as much as you did." Lord Warren walked over to the towering spool of gold with his hands on his hips. "Yes, this'll do just fine."

She shook her head, pushing thoughts of the kiss aside, and tried to focus on the time at hand. She'd been so surprised, she had even forgotten her fear of Lord Warren and two of his bandits entering to evaluate "her" work.

"Then you will let me, and everybody else go now, right?" she said.

He looked at Janice with a smirk on his face. "Is that what you thought we'd do?" He clicked his tongue. "Please, I thought you to be more intelligent than that."

Janice darted her eyes about her, sizing up the large bandits at her side, both awaiting Lord Warren's orders. There was no point in running. She also had no desire to abandon the villagers, either.

Warren stepped close to Janice and leaned in uncomfortably close to her face. "My men and I are taking this money you made and traveling to Wilaldan. And guess what, Miss Wallander? You're coming with us."

Janice's heart dropped to her stomach. If she left with Lord Warren, Ronan wouldn't be able to tell Milly about her predicament on time! And there was no telling if they would be able to find out where she had been taken.

"You look shocked, Janice. Allow me to explain." Warren cracked his knuckles and grinned. The men on either side of her shook with their own gleeful chuckles. "We'd be in a lot of trouble if we stayed here in Polart, so we *have* to leave. And why wouldn't we take our very own gold maker with us?"

Laughter erupted around her, and she felt like she was going to be sick. What were they going to do once they found out she hadn't been the one to spin straw into gold?

Another one of Lord Warren's men burst into the room, tan cheeks red, and his breathing ragged.

"Lord... Lord Warren..." he wheezed.

Warren pushed Janice aside and walked up to the newcomer. "Spit it out! What is it?"

"The King and Queen. They're here!"

# Chapter 15

Janice felt like a boulder had been lifted off of her chest as she heard the news. How had Ronan gotten to Milly and Alexander so quickly? And how did they travel so fast? She shook her head, not caring about all the questions to their arrival. The important thing was, they *did* arrive, and she was saved! Janice's lips twitched into an enormous grin, and this time it was her turn to laugh.

Lord Warren shot her an angry look and ordered the two bandits next to her to restrain her.

"Don't let her out of your sight!" he shouted. Then, gesturing to the man who brought the news, he said, "Let's go!"

Janice struggled from the strong hands gripping her arms— arms so small, their fingers nearly wrapped around them twice.

"Hey!" the one on her right with a nasty scar across his eye growled at her. "You stop that, or I'll hurt you!"

Janice grew stiff but clenched her fists so hard, the blood stopped flowing through her fingers. Lord Warren had a decent amount of men. She just hoped that Milly and Alexander brought more than just a couple of guards and wouldn't be caught by surprise.

The minutes ticked by in slow motion as the three of them stood in the dark room next to a pile of magical gold. The metal sparkled under the candlelight that was about to burn out. Janice was surprised the stub of wax had lasted as long as it did.

The men holding her began shifting uncomfortably.

"Trent, I'm getting really nervous about this," the man with the scar whispered.

Trent, the other, shorter one with a greasy, black mustache nodded quickly. "Me too."

"What if the King and Queen brought an army? All of our comrades might be dead. Sooner or later, they're gonna be searchin' for this one and kill us, too!"

"Colten, you need to calm down!"

Janice's head whipped back and forth from one man to the other as they spoke. And then she had an idea.

"I was thinking," she said, daring to speak, "I bet you still have time to escape. You know, before they find me."

The bandits growled down at her. She flinched involuntarily, but she continued: "This is probably your last chance to save yourselves."

The one named Trent furrowed his brows together and scratched his scruff with his free hand. "I think she might be right."

The other, Colten, paused for a long moment

while tapping the fingers around Janice's arm mindlessly. Then, finally, he nodded in agreement.

"Let's go," Colten said, dropping her arm. Trent followed suit, and both men, without a word to her, grabbed a small pile of gold each, then sprinted out of the room.

Janice rubbed at her numb arms and sighed in relief. She couldn't believe that had worked! Janice shook out her stiff limbs and went in the direction her two captors had, hoping that she could remember how to navigate the manor's halls and to the outside.

After a few wrong turns, she finally found the front door and heaved it open. She squinted her eyes from the morning sun as it sparked an immediate headache— most likely due to entrapment in a dark, dungeon-like room for nearly a day.

The streets were bare, but she knew by now that events usually occurred in the center of town. Hiking up her light blue skirts and muttering under her breath about the castle maids' refusal to let her pack or even *find* simple frocks, Janice took to a run. She was exhausted from an entire night with no sleep, but she was fueled by her eagerness to see Milly and rid Bymead of Lord Warren, and his brutal party of bandits once and for all.

Just as there had been during the bandit attack, there was chaos. But this chaos was welcome to Janice's eyes. There were no burning houses, and the screaming came from Lord Warren's men. The people of Bymead were nowhere to be found, most likely hiding out in their homes as a dozen Polartian guards— in addition to the ones kept prisoner by Lord Warren— flashing the royal colors of deep reds and brilliant purples came upon one bandit after another with swords and spears alike. Janice grinned as she saw a peek of golden hair in the middle of the battle, recognizing her brother-in-law's skilled strikes with his gleaming sword. But where was Milly? Or Ronan?

Janice skirted in the shadows of the buildings to avoid any bandits lingering away from the mayhem. She also couldn't find Lord Warren anywhere. Had he escaped? She couldn't picture him as one to abandon his men, but, then again, she hadn't imagined him to be the criminal he turned out to be, either.

Out of the corner of her eye, Janice saw a barefooted little girl with chestnut hair done into two long, double braids run past her and veer sharply to the left and through a crack in between two homes. Curious, Janice quickened her pace and followed the girl through the narrow passage. After a few tight steps, the path quickly widened into a spacious clearing dotted with short trees. Within the clearing were dozens of villagers, and standing directly in the middle of the admiring group with her shining blonde hair was Milly.

"Jan!" the Queen cried, pushing through the sea of people in front of her.

Tears sprang into Janice's eyes as she met her sister halfway, both of them throwing their arms around each other, sobbing.

"Thank goodness you're alright," said Milly.

Janice's throat tightened from all the tears, but she was able to muster out, "I missed you."

Milly's grip tightened as she dug her pale, button nose into Janice's hair. Janice squeezed her back and felt nearly as relieved to see her sister as the day Milly returned after being kidnapped by King Leopold.

The villagers were watching the scene curiously, but no one moved to interrupt. No one even made a sound.

"How did you get here so fast? Ronan left with the message not two hours ago!"

Milly cocked her head to the side and raised a delicate eyebrow. "Ronan? Who's Ronan? No, Alexander and I received a letter from Regent Edward last week about a bandit raid, and we decided to travel directly to Bymead after the ball in Greriveth." Milly grabbed her sister's hands. "Thank goodness we did! The people here have told me how terrible it has been!"

Janice barely heard what Milly was saying as her thoughts kept turning back to Ronan. "My friend? Did you see him on your way?"

"Was he headed to the capital?"

Janice nodded.

"Then, no. We were coming from Greriveth, and those are completely different roads."

Janice pulled her hands away from Milly's and started wringing them together. If the need for Ronan to travel all the way to Kria was no longer there, then she *definitely* didn't like the idea of him making the trek after a long night of performing draining magic.

Milly noticed her distress and placed a calming hand on her shoulder. "What's wrong? Is he okay?"

Janice's blood began pounding in her ears. Her heart thudded painfully, and her limbs began to grow numb. All of a sudden, the stress of the week in Bymead finally overcame her, and it was like her body snapped. Milly shouted out for help as Janice collapsed onto the grass. Her vision began to blur more and more until finally, everything went dark.

# Chapter 16

The sound of children playing outside slowly woke Janice up from a dreamless sleep. She tried to blink herself awake, feeling incredibly groggy. She ran her fingers along the cotton sheets underneath her, trying to remember where she was. When she did, she bolted upright, immediately regretting it as her head started to pound, and a wave of nausea clenched her stomach into knots.

"You're finally awake!"

Her vision was still blurred, but as it began to clear, she recognized Ronan's glowing face.

"Ronan!" she cried, attempting to reach over to hug him but groaned as she began to see spots.

He held up his hands, brows drawing together with worry. "Whoa. Take it easy. You've been in and out for three days." His eyes scanned her from head to foot. "And you look terrible."

Janice opened her mouth to protest, but the way her body ached suggested she shouldn't argue. She took her turn to scan Ronan, however, recognizing how much better he looked than when she last saw him. He looked to have gained a few needed pounds, and the normal darkness under his eyes was nearly gone. He actually looked… handsome.

Ronan seemed to read her thoughts and chuckled. "Amazing what a few days of good food and not spinning straw into gold can do for someone, eh?"

Janice smiled back but repressed her own chuckles, fearing it would hurt her head even more.

"What happened?" she asked.

Ronan shrugged. "I didn't see anything, but the soldiers— and the King, I hear— defeated the bandits easily, you fainted, were brought to recover in one of the manor's rooms, and I was found knocked out on the side of the road." He wiggled his eyebrows. "Look at the two of us, fainting all over the place."

Janice snorted. "I think we both needed the rest."

She craned her neck to look around the room. It was grand with matching sets of mahogany dressers, a wardrobe, and even the four-poster bed she laid upon. The carpet was inlaid with golden thread, and even the ceiling sparkled with bits of silver.

"So, we're using the manor. I assume that means Lord Warren's been arrested?"

Ronan scowled and clasped his hands together. "Actually, we can't find him."

Janice's heart dropped, but before she could say anything, the door creaked open, and Milly peeked her head in. Milly's bright eyes grew even bigger than they were when she saw Janice.

"Alexander!" she squealed. "She's awake!"

Alexander poked his own head above Milly's

through the crack of the door. The firelight burning near her bed reflected against his round spectacles, and he gave her a gleaming, crooked smile. His smile gave Janice a bit of the warmth she needed after hearing the news about Lord Warren. She had grown to become close friends with her brother-in-law in the past few months, and she was almost as excited to see him as she was Milly.

Both of them rushed over to her bed. Milly jumped on the mattress excitedly, and Alexander clapped his hand on Janice's shoulder. She winced at all the movement, and they raised hands up to their mouths in horror.

"I'm so sorry!" they shouted in unison. Sometimes one could tell they were a married couple deeply in love.

Janice chuckled lightly and squinted her eyes shut protectively against their loud voices. "It's alright. I'm *so* happy to see you both!"

Through the little slits she allowed through her eyes, she could see Ronan starting to back away slowly and out of the room. She sat up to tell him to stay, but he was already gone.

"He sat at your side and didn't leave as soon as we told him of your predicament," Milly said with a gleam in her eye. "And he was in bad shape, too! He was unconscious for a day, asked about you, and then he was in here ever since."

Alexander nodded emphatically as Milly spoke. "Is there something we should know about you two?" he said with a wink.

Janice felt her cheeks grow hot, and she turned her face abashedly into her feather pillow. Milly gasped, and Alexander chuckled.

"Stop," she groaned. "I don't know—I mean... No, I'm not going to tell you."

Milly let a cute giggle slip and nudged her sister lightly in the ribs. "Fine, but you *will* tell me on the way home. You and I will take the carriage, and we'll make Alexander ride horseback."

The King scowled at his wife, but laughter remained in his green eyes. Janice relaxed as she began to appreciate their calming, happy presence. Oh, how she missed them.

"So, I have to ask. What is all this about spinning straw into gold?" Alexander gave her a grave look. The angles in his cheek deepened as he stared intently at her.

Janice gulped. "Well, I—uh—"

Milly held up a hand and laughed. "He's kidding. Ronan explained everything to us."

Janice let out a sigh of relief, then shot an irritated glare at Alexander. He raised his hands up in surrender.

"Just trying to be the King I should be," he teased.

"So, we'll be leaving for Kria in the morning. Now that you're starting to feel better," Milly said, changing the subject. "But right now, we're serving dinner in about two hours. I'm cooking! It has been *so* long since I've been able to do that! Hey, have you seen the dining hall? The image in the glass reminds me so much of Mother."

Janice gave a half-smile at the thought of their lost mother. "I had the same thought when I first met Lord Warren." Her eyes grew wide. "I nearly forgot! Lord Warren! Have you sent any search parties after him?"

Alexander nodded, the severe look on his face real this time. "We did, but no luck. We can only hope that he decides to stay low and not cause any more trouble." His eyes grew dark with anger. "But if we find him, he will be punished severely."

# Chapter 17

Ronan wasn't at dinner. After asking around, no one seemed to have seen him for a while— not since he left Janice's room. She stared at her bowl of chicken soup. While Milly and Alexander assisted her to the dining hall, her appetite was enormous. Not having really eaten for three days was starting to hit her— hard. But now, as she listened to the jovial chatter of the Polartian party, and the melodic laughs of her sister next to her, all she could think about was Ronan, if he had left, and why?

Suddenly, the double doors of the hall burst open and slammed against the walls with a loud bang. It was impressive, too, for Janice knew first-hand how heavy those doors were. The group gasped at the sight of Ronan in the center of the doorway with sweat dripping off his nose, and in his hand, he clutched the collar of Lord Warren. The man was whimpering, his face bloodied from a broken nose, and his tan and gold clothing stained from the blood, as well.

Alexander leapt up so quickly that his chair fell backwards and cracked the stained glass behind him. Both Milly and Janice winced as the crack split all the way through the beautiful depiction of the woman's face. But Janice didn't grieve for long, being too enthralled by the scene before her. Ronan looked so strong. His face glowed radiantly from exertion, and he seemed so *angry* as he threw Warren to the ground and in front of the long dining table.

"How?" Alexander demanded.

Ronan didn't take his burning gaze away from the lord and shrugged. "It pays to be a warlock."

Alexander frowned at the vague answer, but he chose not to push it. "What do you have to say for yourself, Lord Warren?"

Janice and the entire room held their breaths as they awaited his answer. Milly reached a hand over to Janice's and squeezed comfortingly. Lord Warren spat some blood onto the floor, then smiled up at his King.

"I don't, and never will regret anything I did, Your Majesty."

Janice shook her head, then slowly moved her gaze to Ronan. The veins in his neck pulsed, and he looked like he was about to pummel the pathetic man even more than it seemed he already did. Alexander seemed to notice, as well and gave a subtle shake of his head. Ronan took a deep breath, forcing himself to relax, and stepped two steps backward.

"I would work on a better answer, if I were you," Alexander said, his face remaining stoic. "We travel to Kria tomorrow morning, and then we will give you a trial as soon as we are able." The King hooded his eyes and leaned over the table. "But I'm not so sure the jurors will take kindly to you, Lord Warren."

Alexander snapped his fingers, and two guards at the end of the table rushed to the criminal and dragged him out of the dining hall, leaving a trail of blood behind them. Ronan watched them go with a clenched jaw, and as soon as they left, he turned to the King and Queen and gave them a deep bow.

"If I may, Your Majesties, I would like to be dismissed."

Alexander and Milly shared worried glances with each other, then quickly in Janice's direction. Janice sank slightly in her chair.

"Where will you go?" Milly asked.

Ronan stole a glance in Janice's direction but quickly averted his eyes back to the monarchs. " don't know, Your Majesty, but I need a break. I've been through enough for a while."

Alexander studied the young man for a moment but reluctantly gave him a nod. "As you wish, Ronan. On behalf of Polart, we thank you. Are you sure you don't want to stay for some type of reward?"

Ronan laughed, amused by the sentiment. "Oh, no. Breaking that man's nose was reward enough for me."

A wave of laughter echoed through the hall, but Janice couldn't take her eyes off of Ronan. Where was he going? Would she ever see him again? She wanted more than anything to rush to his side and convince him to come back to Kria with them.

With her.

As Ronan gave a final bow and turned to walk away, Janice could feel Milly's accusing stares boring into her.

"What?" Janice said through gritted teeth.

Milly waved her arms dramatically to Ronan as he walked away. "Go after him!"

"Milly, everyone can hear you!" And it was true, all eyes were on the sisters as they spoke.

"I don't care! You love him— I can see it in your eyes!"

"No, I don't!"

Milly pursed her lips and shoved her fists on her hips. "Oh, really? Tell me this: have you kissed him?"

Janice opened and closed her mouth to say no, but she could tell her cheeks were a bright red.

"And how did you feel when you kissed him?"

Janice thought back to that fleeting moment of euphoria. She had felt so safe and warm in his arms, and the kiss they shared, however short, had felt passionate and incredible.

"That's what I thought."

Janice's jaw dropped open. "I didn't even answer!"

Milly gave her a gentle shove out of her seat. "Go. He's getting away."

Janice sighed as she looked at her sister, then Alexander, who seemed to side with his wife as he shooed her along with his hands. Her eyes moved to the open doors that Ronan had disappeared through. She clenched and unclenched her fists anxiously, battling with herself in her mind. Then, without remembering if she told herself to or not, Janice jumped from her chair and squeezed behind all of the people at the table until she made it to the doors and ran after Ronan. Her heart pounded loudly in her ears with nervousness and a touch of excitement, but she could still hear the loud cheers from the entire Polartian party erupting from the dining hall.

# Chapter 18

"Ronan!" Janice screamed into the night as she raced down the streets of Bymead.

A lot of the villagers were in their homes eating dinner with families and sharing their meals with those who had lost their own houses, but a couple passersby still out flashed her confused, questioning looks.

Ronan was a good distance ahead of her and seemed to have not heard her cries, but he was walking at a leisurely pace. Janice hiked up her annoyingly long dress and increased her own speed.

"Ronan," she wheezed. "Ronan, please stop."

He skidded to a halt and turned to face her, a look of surprise etched into his features. "Janice, what—"

She charged him quickly and locked her lips against his. She kissed him urgently, but softly at the same time. Soon, Ronan's fingers ran up Janice's forearms, leaving a trail of goosebumps until they reached her face. They parted for a second, staring intensely into each other's eyes, then Ronan grabbed and kissed her, harder this time. Janice clung to him tightly, as if afraid to let him go.

They pulled apart after their passionate moment

and stared into each other's eyes, lips still so close they touched as both of them smiled.

"I didn't think you felt the same way," Ronan whispered.

"I didn't know I did, but my sister has always been smarter than me."

He raised an eyebrow at that. "Uh, what?"

"Never mind," she said with a laugh, pulling his face to hers once again.

# *Epilogue*

10 years later...

Janice stood on the porch of hers and Ronan's cabin, sweeping away at the bits of pollen from the budding flowers in the forest around them. It was spring-time, and the view of the woods surrounding them was the best that time of year. Well, unless it was fall. The trees grew tall and robust with shining green leaves, and flowers from hundreds of different species bloomed in the grass.

Her daughters loved the flowers the most. During one of Milly's visits, she had taught them how to make necklaces and crowns out of the flowers. It was not something Milly and Janice had ever done as children, not having much of a childhood with a drunken father and a sick mother, but Milly's own daughters learned from the nobles' children in Kria and consequently taught her.

Janice set her broom against the front door and gingerly sat down in the wooden rocking chair Ronan carved for her the week before. He had said he didn't use any spells, but the details in the back were too spectacular for her husband's carpentry skills. Janice placed a hand on her swollen stomach.

"Maybe you'll be a boy," she whispered to her unborn child. "Your two big sisters would love that. Not to mention your father— he would be overjoyed."

Janice turned her gaze back to the field and watched her daughters dance and twirl around the tall grass with their father. Both girls had pale blonde hair like Ronan, but it worked much better on them than him. Ronan himself even admitted it from time to time.

"Mommy!" Sarah, her oldest at ten years old, shouted out to her. "I found a cricket!"

"Let me see! Let me see!" Her five-year-old, little Sophia demanded, tearing at her sister's closed fists. Sarah held her hands high above her head and giggled.

"Don't tease your sister," Ronan scolded, but he laughed along with his girls.

Janice smiled and felt a little tear form in the corner of her eye. She was happy. Truly happy. She had a wonderful husband, three beautiful daughters, and the best part... a cabin. A normal, inconsequential cabin that was only thirty minutes away from her sister by horseback. She could have never imagined life as perfect as it had become.

# Note from the Author

Thank you for taking the time to read my book! I hope you enjoyed it. If you did, spreading the word would be much appreciated! For instance, leaving an Amazon or Goodreads review, or sharing on social media, would make all the difference!

Join my newsletter through my website and receive updates, book releases, and so much more! Site: https://aleesehughes.com

Be sure to follow me on all social medias:
Instagram: @aleesehughes
Facebook: Author Aleese Hughes
Twitter: @AleeseHughes

# Map

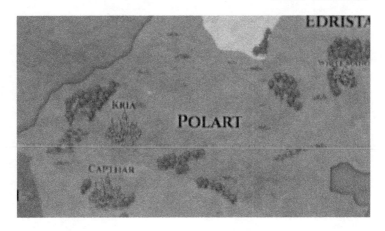

# About the Author

Aleese Hughes is an up-and-coming author with a few books from her *The Tales and Princesses Series* that are out now. She is a loving wife and mother who loves to keep up the home and take care of her daughter, but Aleese also lives and breathes the stage. As a trained singer, dancer, and actress, she has charmed thousands for years. Not many know, however, of her passion for writing. She has always dreamed of being a published author, and now she is living that dream!

# More by Aleese Hughes

## *The Tales and Princesses Series*

Book 1: Peas and Princesses

Book 2: Apples and Princesses

Book 3: Pumpkins and Princesses (Available for Pre-order)

Book 4: Beasts and Princesses: The Story of Bavmorda (Coming in 2020)

Book 5: Beauties and Princesses (Coming in 2020)

## *After the Tales and Princesses*
### *— A Set of Novellas*

Janice Wallander: A Novella Retelling the Tale of Rumpelstiltskin

Queen Dalia Char: A Novella Retelling the Tale of Rose Red (Coming Soon)

CPSIA information can be obtained
at www.ICGtesting.com
Printed in the USA
LVHW090555291019
635549LV00009B/3877/P